THE NEW RECRUIT

D1079556

Titles by Andy McNab:

DROPZONE
Dropzone
Dropzone: Terminal Velocity

BOY SOLDIER (with Robert Rigby)
Boy Soldier
Payback
Avenger
Meltdown

For adults:
Bravo Two Zero
Immediate Action
Seven Troop
Spoken from the Front

Novels:
Aggressor
Brute Force
Crisis Four
Crossfire
Dark Winter
Dead Centre
Deep Black
Exit Wound
Firewall
Last Light
Liberation Day
Recoil
Red Notice
Remote Control
War Torn (with Kym Jordan)
Zero Hour

ANDY McNAB

THE NEW RECRUIT

DOUBLEDAY

THE NEW RECRUIT
A DOUBLEDAY BOOK
Hardback: 978 0 857 53175 9
Trade Paperback: 978 0 857 53176 6

Published in Great Britain by Doubleday,
an imprint of Random House Children's Publishers UK
A Random House Group Company

This edition published 2012

1 3 5 7 9 10 8 6 4 2

With thanks to David Gatward

The Random House Group Limited supports the Forest Stewardship Council (FSC®), the
leading international forest certification organization. Our books carrying the FSC label are
printed on FSC®-certified paper. FSC is the only forest certification scheme endorsed by
the leading environmental organizations, including Greenpeace. Our paper procurement
policy can be found at www.randomhouse.co.uk/environment.

MIX
Paper from
responsible sources
FSC® C016897

Set in Adobe Garamond

RANDOM HOUSE CHILDREN'S PUBLISHERS UK
61–63 Uxbridge Road, London W5 5SA

www.**randomhousechildrens**.co.uk
www.**totallyrandombooks**.co.uk
www.**randomhouse**.co.uk

Addresses for companies within The Random House Group Limited can be found at:
www.randomhouse.co.uk/offices.htm

THE RANDOM HOUSE GROUP Limited Reg. No. 954009

A CIP catalogue record for this book is available from the British Library.

Printed and bound in the UK by Clays Ltd, St Ives plc

For the 2012 intake of Junior Soldiers in
training at Army Foundation College, Harrogate

Thank you for all the help you gave me during
the writing of this book. Without all of you
I wouldn't have been able to ensure that this story
was a true reflection of what you do for our country.
Hopefully it will make you proud of what you
have become. I know I am, and that anyone
who reads this book will feel the same.

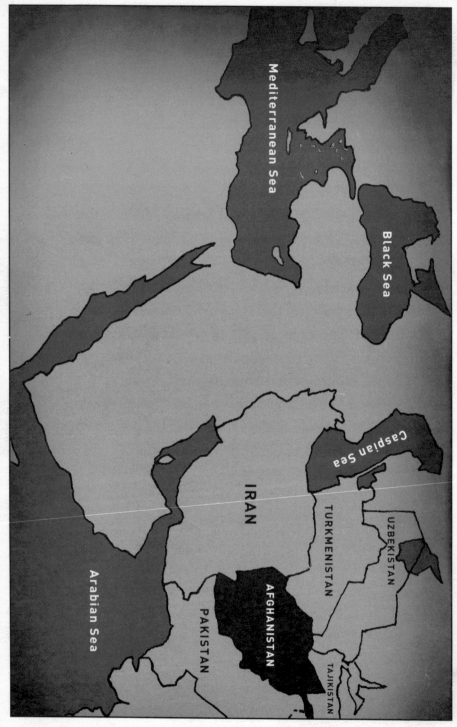

These maps show the approximate location of Afghanistan and Helmand Province in relation to the surrounding areas.

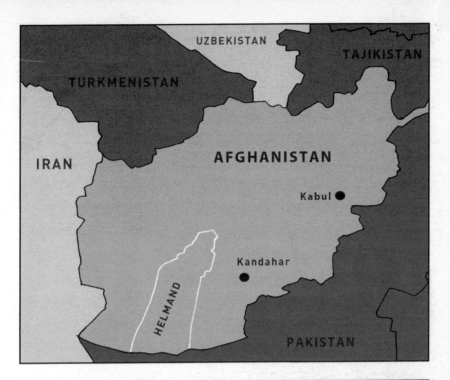

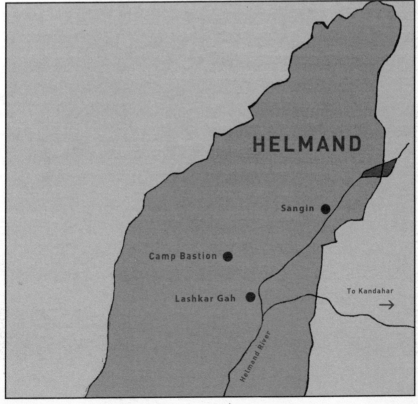

GLOSSARY

50-CAL – Browning M2 machine gun, firing a .50
round and used extensively as a vehicle weapon
and for aircraft armament by the United States
from the 1920s to the present day

AK47 – assault rifle, first developed in the USSR by
Kalashnikov

ammo – ammunition

Apaches – attack helicopters; gunships

ASM – Anti-Structure Munition; a rocket launcher
carrying enhanced explosives to penetrate the
outer wall of a target structure

basha – a shelter, often made in an A-frame shape

BFS – Blank Firing System; used in training to
simulate the noise of live firing and to practise
weapon handling drills

camel pack – a large water reservoir that can be
carried in a soldier's backpack

Camp Bastion – a fortified base for the Coalition

GLOSSARY

Forces in the Helmand Province of Afghanistan

Chinook – helicopter, most often used for transporting equipment or troops; known by soldiers as 'cows'

contact – any action involving the enemy and the discharge of weapons

CSM – Company Sergeant Major

EDIP – Explain, Demonstrate, Imitate, Practise; an Army way of teaching new skills

FOB – Forward Operating Base

GPMG – General-Purpose Machine Gun, nicknamed the 'Gimpy'; belt-driven

Hellfires – missiles predominantly fired by Apache

IED – an Improvised Explosive Device, which can be placed on the ground or used by suicide bombers; sometimes activated by remote control

Infantry – the British Infantry is based on the tried and tested regimental system, which has proved successful on operations over the years; it consists of a number of regular and reserve battalions. The British Infantry has a strong tradition of courage in battle

JDAM – unguided gravity bomb; can have a guidance system bolted on so that it can be guided to a target by GPS

Kevlar – synthetic fibre added to clothing to make it more protective

GLOSSARY

LASM – Light Anti-Structures Missile; a rocket launcher designed to be discarded after launch

LSW – Light Support Weapon

Mastiff – a six-wheel-drive, heavily armoured vehicle

medevac – emergency evacuation of a casualty from a war zone

multiple – group of soldiers numbering approximately 8–12 men

NCO – Non-Commissioned Officer, like a corporal or a sergeant

RPG – Rocket-Propelled Grenade

SA80A2 – semi-automatic rifle made by Heckler & Koch, the standard British Army rifle

sangar – sentry post

SUSAT sight – this gives a 4x magnification and has tritium-powered illumination, thus allowing a soldier to carry on fighting when the light is low at dusk and dawn

Taliban – insurgents/tribal groups fighting for power in Afghanistan, nicknamed 'Terry' by the Army

theatre – field of operations within a war

tour – period of active service; a normal tour in Afghanistan would be approximately six months

Warrior – armoured fighting vehicle

Army Foundation College, Harrogate

'Just do it! Come on, it's a piece of piss.' Liam's own words burned.

Another figure, shaking his head, refusing to budge, ignoring him.

'So you're chicken, then? Is that it?' Liam bent his arms and flapped them like wings.

'Not listening.' Dan's voice was firm as he backed away from Liam, but in the wrong direction. Towards the edge of the building, where they were free running.

'Dan! Stop! The gap!' Liam's stomach turned over as he realized the danger.

A laugh. 'You expect that to work, too? Sort yourself out, Liam. Known you too long, mate.'

Liam shouted again, but still Dan backed away, each step taking him closer and closer to the drop . . .

A scream ripped itself out of Liam's throat. Sitting up,

1

for a moment all he could see was darkness. He was drenched in sweat and his breaths were hard and fast, his heart thumping as though it wanted to burst out of his chest.

Movement . . .

Something was at the end of his bed and the night bent round it as though afraid. Liam had once felt the same, but not any more. Not now. If time hadn't healed him, a life-change had.

'Hey, Liam . . .'

The voice froze the air. Liam's heart was racing now, but it was more due to adrenaline than fear.

A shadowy figure leaned forward. Slowly, deliberately, as though to do so any faster would cause it to topple, collapse, crumble. Its face was a mess of blood and bone, the features barely recognizable, one eye gone, the other wide and staring, unblinking.

Liam breathed deep, squeezed his eyes tight shut, balled the heels of his palms into them till he saw stars, sensed tears slip out to run down his face.

Come on, Liam, sort your bloody head out. It's not there, not real. If you can't handle this then you're going to be no use as a proper soldier!

The shadow was gone.

Lying slowly back in his bed, forcing his breath to slow down, Liam focused on the other sounds in the room. The faint tick of a watch. A bubble of water doing its best to push through a weary heating system. And the deep-sleep breathing of other exhausted young soldiers in the same room.

As he tried to drift back to sleep, he thought of his last days at home, down in London. His mum was in the kitchen, creeping about timidly to make his dad a lunch he wouldn't even eat. His dad, barely sober from the night before – and even in the morning already halfway through another can of Special Brew – was signing the papers for him to enrol at the Army Foundation College in Harrogate.

'So if I sign this, it means you're out of the house for good, right? About fucking time, if you ask me.'

'Just sign it, Dad.'

'What if I don't?'

'For once, don't be an arsehole. And I'll only be home on leave, that's it.'

'You know there's a war on, right?'

'Anything's better than here, Dad.'

And that was it, job done.

Rolling over onto his side, Liam did his best to ignore the pain in his muscles. They hadn't stopped aching from the day he'd arrived.

He checked his watch. With little more than a couple of hours left, he forced his eyes shut.

1

'This place is a shit tip!'

And with that, Corporal McKenzie, a man who made up for being short by being wide and loud and angry, smashed his boot into the bin. It clattered across the floor of the room Liam shared with eleven other junior soldiers, and slammed into the radiator under the window. The sound was deafening.

The corporal came up close enough for Liam to smell his breath. And it wasn't minty fresh. His skin was marked, like he'd spent his childhood picking spots off his face to squeeze out the pus. And the snarl etched into his features, like marks carved into rock, was one worn from pure displeasure.

'Do I need to check your locker, Scott, or shall I just guess that it's a complete bag of bollocks like usual?'

Liam was used to being called by his surname. They all were. It's what they were supposed to call each other when in training or on any exercise. First names didn't count then, mostly because if an officer called out 'Dave' there was a good chance he'd get at least half a dozen 'yes-sir's. That was just annoying; if it happened on the battlefield, it would be downright dangerous.

The corporal edged past Liam, who then heard his locker door open and his kit, which he'd yet again spent ages trying to get just right, heaved out across the floor. His heart sank, but he didn't show it. Corporal McKenzie had a knack of picking up even a flicker of pissed-off in a junior soldier's face. And to him that was just an excuse to come down even harder.

'So what's wrong with you, Scott?' the corporal asked, his voice a loud snarl, bullish and angry, his eyes narrow and piercing. 'Can't you follow simple bloody instructions? Or do you need your mum to come and do it for you? Is that it? A fucking mummy's boy who can't wipe his own arse without having her check it for him?'

Corporal McKenzie held up a laminated sheet of card – the illustrated instructions on how every junior soldier should set out their locker – and shoved it in Liam's face. 'Does your locker look anything like this?'

Of course it doesn't, you bastard, now that you've thrown it all over the floor!

'No, Corporal!'

'What was that?'

Liam said it again, louder.

'Then get it bloody well sorted, Scott. Understand?'

'Yes, Corporal!'

As Corporal McKenzie moved on to deal with the next junior soldier, Liam breathed out slowly. He knew this was all part of getting them into the Army mindset, toughening them up, taking orders, but it was still hard to swallow.

A few minutes later the locker inspection was over.

'He's a right bastard, that one, hey, Scott?' said the bloke opposite.

Liam nodded. It was an accurate description.

The lad who had spoken was Cameron Dinsdale, a seventeen-year-old who hailed from a farm somewhere up north and had a thing for Land Rovers. At first, and because his accent was so thick, Liam had a job understanding just what he was saying. If he lost track he'd already worked out that a nod and a smile was often enough of a response to keep him happy. But the two lads had hit it off immediately, and it felt good, Liam thought, to have a mate.

'It's a height thing,' Cameron added. 'Probably not the only thing that's small, either.'

Liam laughed, along with a few nearby junior soldiers; Cameron seemed to have a knack of cracking jokes at just the right time.

The first few weeks at the Army Foundation College had been non-stop and Liam couldn't remember the last time he'd had any time to himself. If he'd been expecting that Army life would be all running around shooting guns and blowing stuff up, he couldn't have been more wrong. They'd spent as much time in the classroom as they had outdoors, going to lessons, sitting at computers, and working on their reading and writing skills as much as their fitness. Another thing he hadn't been prepared for was that there were girls at the college. Some of them were even pretty fit. Not that he should've been surprised, but a part of him had expected them to be mingers, which they weren't. And some of them, he knew, could probably kick his arse. Now, though, there was a buzz of excitement around the place. In a few hours they were heading off for their first overnight exercise.

'So, you up for this then?'

The question, which was as much a challenge, was from a black lad in the bed next to Liam, Jon Renton. Jon's hands looked like they'd spent years punching their way through walls, his knuckles tough and leathery. He was fit, focused, but always, it seemed, seriously pissed off.

Liam shrugged. They all knew what they had to look forward to. 'Basha building, cooking on a stove and getting shouted at? Yeah, why not?' he said. 'But at least we're outside and not stuck indoors doing basic skills and shit like that, right?'

'Bet it fucking rains,' said Jon, nodding out through the window. 'It's already pissing down. Yorkshire's such a hole. Corporal McKenzie's going to bloody love this, isn't he?'

'Stop putting a downer on everything, Renton, you knob,' said Cameron, who was close to finishing sorting out his locker after the corporal's visit.

Another voice joined in with, 'Yeah, shut it, Renton. You're keeping me awake with all your shit. You're too keen – and too miserable.'

It was Matt Penfold and he was lying on his bed – something he seemed to do a lot. To Liam, he just didn't seem like soldier material. He carried more weight than the rest of them, most of it sort of squishy. With hands the size of dinner plates, he looked more like a truck driver than a bloke who wanted to get tooled up and go head-to-head with the Taliban in the desert.

'It's in the family,' said Jon. 'I've always known I was going to be in the Army – it's a kind of tradition with us. Dad was a Para, which is what I'm aiming for. Grandad did some crazy shit over in France. This is where I belong and I'm not about to let it get fucked up by a lazy twat like you.'

It was a fair point, thought Liam. Penfold was right: Renton was keen; but it hadn't escaped any of them that he was also one of the best at the college.

When the time to head off came round later that day, Liam jumped onto the bus with the others and grabbed a seat by the window. Jon, it seemed, had been right. The rain not only hadn't stopped; if anything, it had got heavier. After a short drive, they were all out of the bus and standing in woodland. Their kit had already been sent ahead, including the SA80s, all the rifles fitted with a bright yellow BFS, or Blank Firing System. Then, after a briefing on what they were going to do, Corporal McKenzie stepped forward.

'The point of this exercise is to give you all a taste of what it's like to live outside. And to see if you can handle being away from a duvet and a hot shower.'

Liam was already cold and wet. So far, so not so good, but he could put up with it, would have to.

'You'll all be sorting out your own shelters and putting up a basha in pairs, cooking up some scoff, doing some simple perimeter patrols. So listen to me and the rest of the staff and don't piss around. You never know, you might surprise us all and learn something.'

A while later, having been split into smaller groups, Liam and the others had watched Corporal McKenzie put a basha up between some trees, explaining everything in detail. Not just the kit involved – a camouflaged waterproof sheet, bungees and some paracord, which were all easily stowed away in your personal kit – but how to find a good spot to pitch camp and how to check it over. Then he'd demonstrated how to put up the basha. It was the same process as always, and one Liam was getting very used to: Explain, Demonstrate, Imitate, Practise, or EDIP for short. Everything they did went through this same sequence, and the construction of the basha had been no different. Now it was their turn.

'And remember,' the corporal had said, finishing off his demonstration, 'keeping your kit dry is absolutely vital. Trust me, from experience, trying to grab some kip in a doss bag that's wet puts a serious downer on the rest of your week. Balls it up and you'll freeze, you won't be able to think straight. And if a firefight kicks off, you'll be no bloody use to anyone.'

Having been put into four-man patrols, Liam and the others were all directed to specific areas to set up camp, each patrol far enough away from the others to at least make the junior soldiers feel like they were out on their own. Liam knew, though, that a member of the staff was always within shouting distance. The only time he didn't feel like he was being watched was when it was lights out, and even then he wasn't so sure.

'Reminds me of home,' said Cameron, sidling up beside Liam. 'Mud, fields and rain. All it needs is a knackered Land Rover with a dead sheep in the back. And my dad swearing through his pipe.'

Liam laughed as they both worked on the process of fixing their basha, just as Corporal McKenzie had demonstrated.

'Don't suppose you've ever seen a tree before, have you?' Cameron asked, once the basha was finally up. 'Being a Londoner, like. Big green and brown thing? Looks a bit like giant broccoli?'

'No, and I don't know where milk comes from either,' said Liam as he set to boiling up some water in his mess tin, over a folding Hexamine stove. He then dropped in a silver food pouch from a twenty-four-hour ration pack they'd all been given to heat it up. A minute later, he ripped it open and tucked in. It was sausage and beans and, if he was honest, didn't taste too bad. A memory flashed into his head: him and his best mate, Dan, as eight-year-olds, trying to cook beans on a smoky fire in Dan's garden. They'd had to scrape them off the pan, but at the time they'd been the best beans he'd ever eaten . . .

'That stuff's rammed with calories,' said Cameron, breaking into his thoughts as he sorted out his own stove. 'Designed to keep you going and to stop you having a shit for at least three days.'

Just opposite, Jon and Matt had finished their own basha. Glancing over, it struck Liam how for the first time since arriving at the college they all actually looked like proper soldiers. They were only four weeks in; but loaded up with kit, drenched, and carrying semi-automatic rifles, they at least looked the part. He wondered briefly what his dad would think if he saw him now. Probably wouldn't care, he thought.

'Who's taking first stag?' asked Cameron a few minutes later as he munched through his own silver pouch of lamb curry.

Liam nodded across at Matt. 'Oi, Penfold – you finished your food first, so you're up.'

Matt protested, but Jon backed him up.

'Shouldn't be such a fat greedy bastard,' he said. 'So quit moaning and do like Liam said: fuck off.'

Liam was stunned. To have Jon agree with anyone was rare.

Matt heaved himself to his feet. 'Someone had better come and get me after an hour,' he said, starting to make his way off to where Liam had set up a lookout point. 'I need my beauty sleep.'

'You're not kidding, Penfold,' said Cameron. 'You're an ugly fucker.'

Food done, and Matt on his way, Liam, like Cameron and Jon, settled down into his doss bag. It wasn't massively comfy, but he was tired, cold and didn't care. He'd be asleep in a second. But when he was woken up by Cameron shaking his shoulder, he wasn't so sure he'd slept at all.

'My turn already?'

Cameron shook his head and Liam could see that for once he wasn't about to crack a funny.

'It's Matt,' said Cameron. 'He's wandered off.'

'But there's nowhere to go!' said Liam. 'We're being observed all the time. And it's not like he's easy to miss, is he? Penfold's huge!'

'He's a fucking muppet,' said Jon, who was standing with Cameron. 'Why the hell is he here, anyway? Just wasting his time and messing stuff up for the rest of us.'

'We're all in the shit if we don't find him,' said Liam, unable to hide his irritation at Matt. 'Losing someone on our first exercise? We'd never live it down!'

'McKenzie will have our balls,' said Jon.

'And wear them as cufflinks,' added Cameron.

'Well, he can't have gone far,' said Liam, still wondering how this could've happened without someone like Corporal McKenzie coming over, with a cowed-looking Matt in front of him, to find out how they'd already managed to screw things up so badly. 'Let's sweep the area till we find him.'

Taking care with each footstep not to get caught in a

tree root or slip on a rock, Liam walked through the dark, with Cameron and Jon to each side. Despite the fact that what they were now doing could end up getting them all in serious trouble if they didn't find Matt, it was the first time Liam had felt like he was on his way to being a proper soldier. Edging through the darkness of the trees, it was easy to imagine what it would be like out on a proper patrol. The thought excited him and made him nervous. This was just a night out in a wood searching for an idiot who cast a shadow as big as Ben Nevis. It didn't compare to going out on foot patrol in Afghanistan, where the Taliban were waiting in ambush to riddle you with bullets or blow you apart with an IED.

'When we find him, I'm going to break his legs,' said Jon, his face stern. 'Even if I have to use a sledge-hammer.'

Liam understood the sentiment; he was up for giving Matt a kicking as well. But just then he heard something: an odd rumbling, breathing sound, like a paddling pool deflating.

'Over there,' he said, and motioned for the other two to follow. A few metres on they all spotted Matt at the same time. He was flat out on the ground and fast asleep, his rifle at his feet.

Liam went over and sent a hefty kick into Matt's

thigh. 'What the hell are you doing? You're in the wrong sodding place, Penfold! Bloody useless, or what?'

'Look, I'm sorry, lads,' said Matt, clambering to his feet.

'Sorry wouldn't mean shit if we were out in Afghanistan and you let the Taliban past to slot us!' said Jon.

'Never mind the Taliban,' said Cameron. 'What about Corporal McKenzie?'

'*What about me?*'

Liam froze. They all did.

'A word,' said the corporal as he slipped out from the shadows. 'Not a great start, is it, lads?'

Just as Liam had suspected, someone had been watching them all along. And it just had to be Corporal McKenzie, didn't it?

'Let's just say you're all bloody lucky this is just an exercise.'

A moment's silence, like Corporal McKenzie wanted them to think about each and every word he was saying.

'A man goes missing? That's serious,' he said, eyeballing them one by one, his voice rising. 'This isn't a bloody Cub Scout camping trip! What if this happened in theatre? What if one of you walked off and got lost, tripped an IED, or got captured?'

No one said a word.

'Anything like this happens again, you'll be in serious trouble,' said the corporal. 'Understand?'

Liam and the others responded with a sharp, 'Yes, Corporal.'

Corporal McKenzie said nothing more, turned, and marched off, his presence replaced by a thick, heavy blanket of ominous quiet.

Cameron broke the silence. 'Renton?'

'What?'

'You were right about the balls.'

2

The brick building had no windows, no way out at all except for the solid metal door now in front of them. It was the second half of the first term and Liam was lined up with a group of other junior soldiers on a rare bright day, his stomach twisting itself like steel rope. He was getting used to the sensation of having to deal with his nerves when faced with doing something new, but this time, more than any other yet at the college, he was really feeling it.

Dressed in his combats, he was also carrying a respirator. They'd all practised putting the respirators on, getting them to fit snug to the face, and they'd even worn them round the assault course, which had been no fun at all. Liam had soon discovered that running while wearing a respirator was horrific: they were made of rubber and stuck to your face, and no one had warned them that the only way to get rid of the build-up of sweat inside the mask was to drink it.

'You all know why you're here,' said Corporal McKenzie. 'CS gas is something you all have to experience so that you know what it feels like and how to deal with it. Also, it gives me a bit of entertainment.'

Liam wasn't so sure about the whole 'need to experience it' aspect of what they were about to do. Earlier that day, junior soldiers had been chatting about how the CS gas experience was going to be a right laugh, and betting which one of them was going to choke first, even pass out. Breathing in gas sounded horrific and he just wanted it over and done with.

Since the run-in with McKenzie after Matt had gone missing on the night exercise, Liam and the others had worked hard and kept their heads down. The weeks were mostly flying by. Locker inspections had gradually become less stringent and they were all getting fitter by the day. Liam now knew how to wear his uniform without getting bollocked for something being in the wrong place, he could march, and his basic skills were improving day by day, as was his ability in the classroom. He even had a good knowledge of how to strip and clean an SA80 and could survive on less sleep than he'd ever thought possible. He was actually enjoying pretty much everything he was doing. Now, though, he had a feeling that this was about to change.

'To recap,' said Corporal McKenzie, 'CS gas, or tear gas as it's also known, is used for riot control. And trust me, it really works. Fire a can of this stuff into a crowd and they're yours.'

Liam had heard this already, as had they all, but the corporal was obviously enjoying laying it on thick.

'The chemical reacts with moisture, be it sweat on your skin, the water in your eyes, saliva in your mouth, snot up your nose.'

Yep, thought Liam, it still sounded absolutely fucking dreadful.

'You'll feel a burning sensation and your eyes will shut automatically. Nothing you can do about it. So you'll be blind.'

The corporal paused, and Liam had no doubt that it was for dramatic effect.

'Next, you can expect all or any of the following: your eyes will stream with water, you'll cough like you've something stuck in your throat; mucus and snot will pour out of your nose, your eyes and throat will burn like they're on fire, and you might even throw up. You'll be disorientated, dizzy, and unable to breathe. And there is no backing out. Everyone does this. And I know most, if not all of you, don't want to.'

His piece said, Corporal McKenzie walked over and opened the door to the brick building.

'I'm going to call you in by name. File in, line up, shut up. Scott!'

Liam was relieved. Being called first at least meant he'd have it all over and done with before anyone else.

Inside, the brick building was as plain as it was on the outside. It was an oppressive place, dark and damp, and the air was stale, with an acrid tang to it that stuck in the back of his throat.

Another junior soldier lined up next to him. It was Cameron, but neither of them spoke. A nod was enough. They were too focused on what they were about to go through. Then came Matt, Jon and the others. Silently they stood in a line, like they were waiting for a firing squad.

Corporal McKenzie strode in, shutting the door behind him. The only light getting into the room now was through a grubby skylight that wasn't really up to the job thanks to the amount of bird crap on it.

'In a moment,' began the corporal, 'CS gas will be released in this room. After that, I will call you in turn. You must then take off your respirator. And to stop you attempting to hold your breath, you will call out as clearly as you can your name, rank and number. Do you understand?'

'Yes, Corporal!'

'Good. Now, respirators on!'

Liam ignored his heart, which was now racing and hammering hard at the inside of his ribcage, and pulled on his respirator. It stuck to his face immediately. He checked it like he'd been shown, to make sure there was no way for any air to get in except through the filter. Already, the eye visors were steaming up, making visibility, if possible, even worse. Breathing just added to the problem, and he couldn't just hold his breath for the next ten minutes.

When Corporal McKenzie released the CS gas, then a few moments later called out the first name, Liam realized something. First in meant last out. He was going to have to stand here and listen to all the others rip off their respirators, choke and splutter, before he got to have his turn.

His heart thumped harder.

The first junior soldier to have his name called out ripped off his respirator and spoke, but he barely got his surname out before the coughing and choking became too much for him and he was through the door. Liam hadn't seen it, hadn't dared move, but he'd heard it and that had been enough. It had sounded like a man dying, choking on his own vomit, drowning in his own spit.

The next junior soldier, a girl whose thick Brummy accent had made it almost impossible for Liam to understand a word she said, fared much the same, though after pulling off her respirator she at least managed to get through her full name before faltering and collapsing to her knees. Liam turned his head just enough to see what was happening and saw her being pulled to her feet by Corporal McKenzie and pushed out through the door. It was, in an odd way, comforting to see that the NCOs weren't any easier on the girls. Everyone here was treated the same and that was the point, thought Liam. Didn't matter what sex you were: make the grade, or sod off, simple as that.

And so it continued, with one after another after another taking off their respirator, attempting to speak, being hit by the CS gas, then collapsing into a fit of coughing and spluttering and panic. By now, Liam's own respirator was doing what it seemed to do best, making his face overheat, causing him to sweat. Drips of the stuff were sliding down his cheeks, and pooling around the edge where the respirator gripped at his face.

Jon's name was called. He lasted no longer than any of the others, and was pushed out of the door a few seconds after saying his name.

'Penfold!'

Liam caught a flicker of movement as Matt heaved his respirator from off his face. He didn't even manage to get his name out before coughing so hard that the force of it sent him forward and down onto his face with such violence that Liam couldn't help but wince.

Corporal McKenzie called for help from another corporal, and they quickly helped the stumbling, spluttering mess that was Matt out of the room and back into the outside world.

'Dinsdale!'

Liam saw his mate rip his respirator off, heard him say his name, then that was it. Cameron's eyes snapped shut. He coughed like his lungs were trying to get out through his mouth. Snot burst from his nose and he doubled over. Then he was grabbed by the corporal and marched out through the door.

Liam was the only one left. He stood waiting for his name to be called while Corporal McKenzie stared at him. Why the hell wasn't he calling his name out? What was going on? Was he trying to mess with him? If he was, it was working.

'Scott!'

As if a switch had been flicked, Liam had torn the respirator from his face almost before he'd realized what he was doing. He opened his mouth to speak but instead took a huge breath. It was like sucking in a petrol bomb as the match was lit. His insides felt like they were burning up. Then his face reacted, his eyes slammed shut, and his nose started to seep snot. He couldn't see, couldn't breathe. If he tried to suck in air, his nose closed up, or he just sucked more mucus and saliva down his throat. Panic squeezed him. Snot and mucus poured from his nostrils. He was going to die! He knew it! No way could he survive this. He was going to pass out, stop breathing, and that would be it, game over.

Fuck . . .

Liam felt a shove in his back and he stumbled forward, only just managing to stop himself falling, then a bright light crashed into his barely open eyes. He was outside, but the CS gas was still working on him. He breathed fresh air, but it only made it worse, like drinking a beer after a hot curry. He doubled over, coughed, spat, pulled great streams of slimy shit out of his nose. He tried to stand up straight, but he still couldn't see well; he was disorientated and stumbled sideways into a metal bin. It clattered to the ground, the sound ringing like a church bell in his ears. Hands grabbed him, helped him stand, and at last the burning sensation started to subside.

Liam, his eyes now able to open, blinked at the brightness of the day. For a moment, he still couldn't focus properly. When he did, Cameron was in front of him, checking he was all right, watching his back as they had begun to do during exercises.

'Penfold's fucked,' he said, nodding behind him.

Liam turned to see what Cameron was on about.

Matt was sitting on the grass, his face racked with pain. A corporal and another member of staff was with him, checking him over and bandaging up one ankle. They'd left his boot on, as there was no point taking it off yet; it was still providing support and would do so until they got him back to the college medical centre.

'What happened?' Liam asked.

'Looks like his ankle's broken,' said Cameron. 'Not confirmed, but with the noise he's making I can't see that it'll be anything else. You know what that means, don't you?'

'Possible medical discharge,' answered Liam.

'Probably a good thing anyway,' said Cameron. 'Never really been able to work out what the hell he was doing here in the first place. Penfold's a lazy sod.'

A stretcher arrived and everyone watched as Matt was carried off. Then Corporal McKenzie ordered them all to line up.

'I'm not going to bother asking how that was for you all, because I know the answer: it was shit, right?'

Liam and the others all nodded. Some were still coughing, including Liam; his eyes were still watering and his nose running like he'd got the worst cold in years.

'You experienced it for just a few seconds and it knocked you all flat,' said McKenzie. 'Now think how effective it is in a crowd where you can't escape from it, and not just one but half a dozen canisters have been thrown at you.'

That evening, back in their room, Liam and the others had still heard no word about Matt.

'He's going to be binned,' said Jon. 'Everyone saw him tumble. His ankle must be a mess.'

A shadow fell across the floor.

'Evening, lads.'

At the sound of Corporal McKenzie's voice, everyone in the room stood to attention.

'Just thought you should know that Penfold's bust his ankle. It's a medical discharge. He can come back when it's mended if he still wants to, but for now he needs to let it heal.'

And that was it; no more was said, and McKenzie left the room.

For a moment, silence reigned.

'One down,' said Cameron, slumping onto his bed.

'He was weak,' said Jon. 'Bloody waste of space, Penfold. Always had it coming. Amazed he made it this far. But we can hack it, right?'

'Yeah, we're nails,' said Cameron, smiling, but also a little serious, if not confidently so.

Liam liked the sense of camaraderie. With Matt

binned, it seemed as though the three of them were suddenly pulled closer together.

'Three to go,' he finished, and remembered his dad signing the papers, half drunk. He had nothing to go home to; there was no future back there, of that he was absolutely sure. Liam knew he had to see it through to the end and finish the course. Become a soldier.

3

Walking to the firing range, Liam went through a quick mental recap of everything they'd been taught, and everything they'd learned, both in the classroom and on the 25-metre range, about the British Army's SA80 A2, the semi-automatic rifle they would all be carrying in active service. He particularly remembered how Corporal McKenzie had clearly enjoyed telling them the fabled story about the weapon being so accurate when it was introduced that the Army marksmanship tests had to be redesigned. As for the technical stuff, it was a cinch. He knew it off by heart. Now they were in their second term, they all did.

Made by Heckler & Koch, the SA80 was a semi-automatic rifle that fired 5.56mm ammunition from a 30-round magazine. It was fitted with the world-famous SUSAT sight, which gave a 4x magnification and had tritium-powered illumination, so a soldier could carry on fighting when the light was low, at dusk and dawn. The SA80 could be fitted with an under-slung grenade launcher, was accurate out to 400 metres, and the user could select single-shot, three-round bursts, or fully automatic mode with just a flick of the change lever. And one thing that had been drilled into them from the off was that on the range they'd only ever use the weapon on single-shot mode, period.

'Anyone here thinks they can go all *Die Hard* on me and empty a full magazine into a target on automatic had better just fuck off now,' the corporal had bellowed at them while demonstrating the change lever. 'You ever find yourself in a position to use one of these on full-auto, then you'll be fighting for your life anyway, so go right ahead. But here, on the range? Don't even think about it. Chances are someone will get hurt. And by hurt, I mean have their bollocks shot off. Understand?'

'Yes, Corporal,' they had shouted back.

The lessons on the SA80 back in the first term had all been classroom-based, covering the basics of the weapon: how to strip it, clean it, all the technical stuff that the Army wanted to make sure every junior soldier got right before they were allowed to pull a trigger for real.

In the classroom, Corporal McKenzie had sat opposite them, an SA80 cradled in his hands like it belonged there. To Liam, it had seemed as though the corporal was trying to drill his stare into every single junior soldier in front of him, to make sure he had their absolute and undivided attention.

'This is your personal weapon. You must become skilled in its use to kill all enemy on the battlefield. It is as simple as that. Got it?'

Liam remembered how the corporal had emphasized the word *personal*. Like he wasn't just saying this weapon was yours to keep, but that you'd better look after it or you're dead and it'll be your own fault.

As one, the junior soldiers had all replied with, 'Yes, Corporal.'

'Well, that's something.'

Corporal McKenzie had then gone through the process of stripping the weapon, pointing out the main components as he went, until the rifle was laid out in pieces in front of him.

'From the live end of the weapon: muzzle and flash eliminator. Trigger, trigger housing, safety catch . . .'

Now, in their second term, and out at the range, Liam mouthed the words himself, mentally rehearsing everything they'd been shown. He was confident that the information was hammered securely into his memory, but it didn't stop him going through it one more time. He still wanted to make absolutely sure he wasn't about to lose any of it.

Arriving at the firing range, Liam sat down on a bench next to Jon and Cameron. About fifty metres in front of them was a crop of half a dozen man-shaped paper targets pinned to plywood boards, behind which rose a steep and high bank of mud. It was twice the distance they'd fired from before and it looked it. Standing on the firing line, between the junior soldiers and the targets, were Corporal McKenzie and a few of his fellow NCOs. And, after McKenzie had come over and given them the expected safety talk, delivered like he was already bollocking them for something none of them realized they'd actually done, it was time for them to step up and lay down some rounds.

Liam watched as the first group were all called out. Each of them grabbed a pair of ear defenders, then walked out onto the range and up to the firing line where McKenzie was now back with the other corporals. After a regimented run-through of the final obligatory checks, the junior soldiers held their weapons parallel to the ground and, on Corporal McKenzie's orders, prepared to open fire.

The crack of the bullets bounced around the range as the rounds burst from the barrels of the rifles and slammed into the targets. Liam was by now itching for his own turn, could barely wait. He knew as well as anyone that soldiering wasn't just about weapons and fighting, but then neither was it all about running across logs or learning to iron a crease in a pair of trousers. And it certainly wasn't anything like any of the Army adverts he'd seen on television. It was all of this, and more, but there was something electrifying about using a weapon. It was as if it focused everything they'd learned, made it all make sense. Whatever it was, Liam wanted to get out on the range.

A few minutes later, their rounds spent and accuracy analysed for good or bad, the first group of junior soldiers finished and Liam, with Cameron, stood up and walked towards the firing line. He adjusted his helmet, making sure his ear defenders were comfortable, then, as with the group before, under orders from Corporal McKenzie, he and the other junior soldiers readied their weapons.

In that moment the rifle seemed to Liam to increase in weight tenfold. It wasn't a physical weight, though, but a realization that the only reason to ever use it was to kill another human being. The SA80 was built to kill and to do so effectively and with unmatched accuracy and efficiency. It was hard and cold, with a deadly purpose. And its reputation was almost unmatched in theatre, even when pitted against one of the most recognizable semi-automatic rifles in the world, the AR-15, or M16 as most people knew it.

Liam stared at the target ahead of him, the SUSAT drawing it just close enough to give him a clear view of what he was aiming at. The cool wind, which had been light and refreshing as they'd made their way out to the firing range, was now heavy and angry.

'Standing position,' Corporal McKenzie called out. 'Ten rounds, in your own time.' Then he roared at them with a simple two-word charge that brought Liam's senses on line like a spark lighting a touchpaper: 'Go on!'

Liam, his weight forward on his left foot, as the corporal had demonstrated, gently squeezed the trigger. The weapon jolted hard in his hands, bucking against him, the recoil mechanism forcing the stock to thump hard into his shoulder. He gripped even harder, worried it might bounce out of his grip, crash to the ground, and let off a stray round to smash the back out of another soldier's head. The SA80 was lethal, and if he didn't control it properly it could just as easily bite him on the arse. Or shoot his face off.

Liam stared at the target. It looked undamaged. Wherever he'd just fired, it clearly hadn't been where he had been aiming. He was annoyed – he didn't like getting things wrong, certainly not things like this, things that seriously mattered. Things that other people were watching you do.

Corporal McKenzie came alongside and Liam noticed that the usual pit-bull snarl had been replaced by one of calm and focus. Corporal McKenzie, Liam had come to realize, was an odd mix of unbridled rage and detailed, careful coaching, and Liam listened to his every word. The shouting, the yelling, the endlessly picking them up on the tiniest thing wrong, was all for their own good.

'You nicked it, and that's something,' the corporal said, as Liam stared at his target. 'You'll improve. Just remember to never snatch at the trigger; *squeeze* it. And after you take a shot, try what I do: lower your weapon, control your breathing, then come back up for your next shot. That way you're not just fixed in that aiming position all the time.'

Liam and the rest of the junior soldiers understood that Corporal McKenzie didn't want them making any mistakes. And neither did he want any of them going up against a hostile force without the right skills to take them on and win.

'Means your arm muscles don't get tired,' continued the corporal. 'And you maintain focus. That in turn means you can get proficient, accurate, can protect yourself and your mates and slot any bastard who wants to come in and have a go. Understand?'

'Yes, Corporal.'

Corporal McKenzie gave a nod and moved down the line.

Liam, following the corporal's instructions, squeezed off another shot. The crack of the bullet was dulled by the ear defenders clamped over his skull, but it wasn't any less frightening to hear the live round blast from the weapon in his hands. This time, though, any fear was displaced just a little by his excitement. And with this second shot, he could see, he'd hit the target!

Liam grinned. This part of the experience had never been mentioned: that to fire a weapon was actually fun. All they ever heard was how to do things right, never what something might really feel like. And here and now, as he fired another round, Liam found that he was enjoying himself. And the adrenaline racing through him took him back, way back to his time with the lads, when free running around the London cityscape was all any of them did. He couldn't help but think how much Dan would have enjoyed this if they could have joined up together . . .

Another shot, then another. Liam's grin widened. The adrenaline was really flowing now; he could sense the tingle of it in his fingertips, the thrill growing.

He glanced over to Cameron, who was focused on the task in hand, head down, staring through the sights, firing the weapon. He looked a natural.

THE NEW RECRUIT

Liam came back on line to fire his own weapon, and as he did so he caught sight of the change lever and his mind seemed to seize up for a moment. He couldn't remember if it was in the right position or not. The thing was marked, but right then, it meant nothing to him. He tried to focus, sort his mind out, but all he could think was: what if it wasn't right and he still went and fired? What then?

At the sound of Cameron putting down another two rounds, Liam flicked the lever to what he thought was almost certain to be the right setting. And then he pulled the trigger.

4

The weapon exploded into life as the magazine emptied in seconds and Liam swore, his voice drowned out as the target in front of him was peppered with holes, the rounds slamming home at a rate of over 600rpm. The shock of it knocked him back, almost made him stumble.

Magazine empty, the world fell silent and Liam lowered his weapon. Adrenaline was coursing through him from what he'd just done.

The next thing he knew, his weapon had been taken from him, his ear defenders ripped from his head, and Corporal McKenzie was right up in his face screaming at him, spit flying everywhere.

'What the fucking hell do you think you're doing, Scott?'

Liam didn't quite know how to respond, was still stunned by just how quickly the bullets had left the barrel.

'Who gave you the order to switch to fully automatic?'

Liam opened his mouth to say something, to explain that it was an accident, but Corporal McKenzie jumped in first.

'You going to fucking well answer me, Scott, or just stand there like a big heap of shit?'

'It was—'

'I'll tell you what it was,' the corporal interrupted, shutting Liam down. 'It was you disobeying a direct order and putting your life, *and ours*, at risk! Have you any idea just how much fucking damage a 5.56 round, travelling at 940 metres per second, can do to a human head at point-blank range? Well, have you?'

Liam remained quiet. The corporal, not so much.

'Do you have any fucking idea how dangerous what you just did was? Any idea at all? Or are you just a fuckwit who's been lucky to get this far? Well?'

Liam understood what the corporal was saying. How could he not? But he hadn't done it on purpose.

'I got confused,' said Liam, realizing immediately just how lame his excuse was going to sound. So he snapped his mouth shut before anything else idiotic fell out of it.

Corporal McKenzie leaned in even closer to Liam's face, so close that their noses nearly touched.

'If you did that on purpose, Scott, it's a chargeable offence, did you know that?'

Liam shook his head. 'No, Corporal.'

'I'm not going to bother explaining it to you here,' continued McKenzie, 'but let's just say if that was proved to be deliberate, you'd be so deep in the shit you'd have to swim to stop yourself from drowning in it.'

Liam tried to swallow, but his mouth, his throat, was dry.

'Get back with the others,' finished the corporal. 'And I want you in my office as soon as we return to barracks, got me?'

Liam nodded.

'I'm sorry, Scott, I didn't hear you . . .' McKenzie growled.

'Yes, Corporal!' shouted Liam.

He didn't wait for any more chit-chat and did as the corporal had said. Sitting back with the other junior soldiers as another group stood to take their turn at the firing range, Cameron squeezed in next to him.

'Scott, mate, that was fucking awesome! Can't believe you did that!'

Liam looked at his mate and saw a huge smirk on his face. 'Yeah, it was, wasn't it?' he agreed, and tried a smile. It didn't sit quite right on his face and he really hoped he hadn't completely shagged things up. 'Though I reckon McKenzie doesn't think so, eh?'

Another figure appeared in front of Liam. It was Jon.

'You're a right fucking idiot, Scott,' said Jon. 'McKenzie's going to skin you when you get back. And do it really slowly too.' Then he added, 'Ballsy, though, I'll give you that.'

'What did it feel like?' asked Cameron. 'I mean, you emptied the mag, Liam! It was fucking out there, mate!'

McKenzie and the last group of recruits came back from the firing line, and then they were all marching back to barracks. When they were dismissed, Liam allowed himself for a second to think that Corporal McKenzie had forgotten what had happened, but then a familiar voice crashed into his ears: 'Scott, you little shit! My office! NOW!'

As Liam marched over to follow Corporal McKenzie, doing his best to try not to think what punishment was going to be meted out on him, he spotted Cameron and Jon. Together, and out of eyesight from the corporal, they stood to attention, and saluted him.

A few minutes later, he was standing rigidly in front of Corporal McKenzie's desk, the corporal having gone off and left him alone. The room was sparse, tidy, gave nothing away as to what lay beyond the corporal's military exterior. Liam couldn't see a photo of a wife or any family, not even one of a pet dog. Not that he'd seen the office of any of the other NCOs, but when he'd first been in there he'd at least expected some hint of what, for Corporal McKenzie, was in his life beyond the Army.

It was some time before McKenzie returned, and when he did, Liam, who was still standing to attention, had almost lost all sensation in his legs.

McKenzie sat down. He did it, Liam noticed, with the weight of a man about to deliver the death sentence.

'I could have you kicked out,' he said. 'Still might, for that stupid prank you pulled out there today. I've seen some stupid things happen in my time here, Scott, but that was something else. What have you got to say to that?'

Liam said, 'It was an accident, Corporal. A misjudgement.'

McKenzie was out of his seat, round his desk and in Liam's face in a moment.

'A misjudgement? Are you fully fucking serious? I mean, are you telling me that you have the actual balls to stand there and try and fob me off with some shit excuse that it was just a mistake? What the hell do you take me for?'

Liam kept his answer simple, tried to make sure his voice didn't falter, despite the fact that he was now bricking it big-time. 'Yes, Corporal. It's the truth, Corporal.'

Corporal McKenzie continued shouting. 'What you did out there was the most idiotic display of incompetence I have ever witnessed, you hear me?'

Liam didn't respond, couldn't think of anything to say, because all he was worried about now was that he was about to be binned. And that terrified him.

Corporal McKenzie stared up at Liam for a moment more, then swung back round to his seat and sat down.

'Fuck knows why, Scott,' he said at last, 'but I'm not going to kick your sorry arse out. Not yet, anyway. I've already spent too much of my own time and effort, and tax payers' money, into making you a soldier, so I'm not going to see that going to waste.'

Liam wanted to punch the air with relief, but he knew Corporal McKenzie definitely wouldn't appreciate it. Also, the corporal hadn't quite finished what he was saying.

'But that doesn't mean I'm going to let you get away with the stupidest fucking display I've ever seen in my life. So you'll see the boss, who will deal with you.'

Liam said, 'Yes, Corporal.'

'He might fine you. I don't know how much,' continued the corporal, leaning forward to rest his elbows on his desk, 'but I can assure you it'll sting. Why? Well, let me tell you why, Scott.' He paused, but only to take one long, deep breath. 'I want you to remember this moment, Scott. I want you to remember, for the rest of your Army career, that I decided to give you a second chance. Because believe me, if I get even a *sniff* of you messing something else up, I'll personally kick your sorry arse back into civvy street so hard my bootprint will serve as a permanent reminder of just what a bastard I can be! Now get the fuck out of my office!'

Liam didn't need to be told twice.

5

The final term, just like the others, pushed on despite the weather. The sky was black and rain was hammering the ground into submission. Corporal McKenzie was, unlike the junior soldiers in front of him, protected from the worst the weather could chuck at him by a worn-looking but still effective Gore-tex combat jacket. They were standing out on one of the concrete roads that snaked in and around the college.

'As you've got leave coming up,' the corporal shouted, 'what better way to finish a term than to do a little bit of exercise?'

No one laughed; no one said a word.

'You need to show us that you're fit enough to deal with all that Army life will throw at you. And throw it at you it will.'

Staring ahead into the rain, the water blurred Liam's vision, but he was still able to make out the silhouettes of Cameron and Jon. When it came to what they were about to do, it was every man and woman for themselves. Liam had beaten Cameron a few times, but Jon not once. He wanted that record to change today.

He was soaked to the skin, the rain coming down in stair rods, but he didn't care. Hot weather made him sweat, the cold made him freeze, and if it was windy, he was either fighting against it or trying to stop it knocking him off his feet. Running in the rain, though, kept him cool. It refreshed him, kept him going.

Corporal McKenzie spoke again. 'You've all done your fitness tests, the press-ups and sit-ups, and passed them. Now you've all got to hammer out a decent time for the one-and-a-half-mile run in under ten and a half minutes. If your fitness isn't up to scratch, you could get back-termed. So let's get to it!'

Corporal McKenzie stepped back, to be replaced by the PTI, the physical training instructor, a man whose physique was based, it seemed, on the design of a tank.

'I don't want any foot draggers,' said the PTI. 'All any of you should be thinking about is getting round this as fast as possible. It's just a few minutes of your life. So make them count. Focus and push yourselves! You can do this!'

Liam, like the rest of the junior soldiers, was silent,

his mind on what he had to do now. He wasn't going to fail at this. He'd worked hard on his fitness, even spent his last two-week leave doing little else but train, eat well and sleep. Even if it was just to get him out and away from his parents, particularly his dad, who didn't seem exactly happy to have him back.

Now he simply had to put all that hard work to good use. And if that meant throwing up halfway round the course to make sure he made it, he didn't care.

Liam calmed his breathing, imagined himself running, racing ahead, his feet pounding hard, his muscles working like engine pistons, firing him forward.

The PTI's voice cut through the air: 'Go!'

Like a foxhound at the sight of its quarry, Liam, in amongst the rest of the junior soldiers, launched himself forward, battling to keep on his feet as the great mass of drenched teenagers raced off.

The ground was slippery thanks to the rain, and Liam had to work hard not only to keep his pace up, but also to stop himself slipping and twisting his ankle. Ahead of him, a female junior soldier called Taylor went down. It wasn't an easy fall to get up from either. She'd gone down hard, but was up on her feet sharp, her knees grazed and bleeding. The PTI looked to check she was OK, but Taylor was already speeding off, the limp doing nothing to slow her down.

Liam kept on moving, thinking only of that stop-watch timing him, almost like it wanted him to fail. And sometimes it seemed like it did. Some days, the fitness stuff was beyond him and he'd be blowing out of his arse within minutes, the PTIs yelling at him. Other days, like today, he'd be on fire. And that always felt good.

A college building sped past, a car park, then another building, a great grey blur that Liam ignored as he pushed on. He was giving no thought to pacing himself, to starting easy and finishing hard. None of that was important. Just the finish line and getting there as fast as possible. And the only way to achieve that was to dig deep and keep his legs pumping hard.

Jon's voice yelled out from behind: 'Come on, Scott! Move it! Fuck me, are you slow!'

In a moment he was right beside Liam and running like a gazelle, hardly out of breath. Liam couldn't see Cameron, but neither was he about to go looking for him. Sure, they watched each other's backs, but when it came to situations like this, each needed all his focus on his own performance. NCOs were watching. And sometimes Liam wondered if they wanted them to screw up.

Jon pushed on past, and all that did was to stir Liam to blank out any pain that was telling him to stop, to ignore it completely and just crash on through to the end.

The junior soldiers were thinning out now, the slower ones gradually falling behind. Liam wasn't going to be one of them – he had Jon in his sights and that was pulling him forward.

At the halfway point, he pushed on with a fresh burst of energy, fired up that he was still powering on. His instincts told him that he was on target to smash his previous time. If he could just do this in under ten minutes . . .

Ahead, Liam saw vomit exploding out of someone's mouth to land on the grass at the side of the road. It didn't stop them running. Liam had seen it happen before. Hell, it had nearly happened to him, but he'd managed to swallow it back down before chucking up later all over his kit.

A corner came up fast. As Liam made to zip round it, his foot skidded across the road, then twisted out from under him. He heard something grind or snap, he wasn't sure, but there was nothing he could do to stop himself slamming into the ground.

Pain raced up his leg, made him yell out. Junior soldiers came at him and he covered his head, ducking to avoid getting kicked in the face as light exploded in front of his eyes like his vision had been blown to pieces by a shotgun blast. He swore.

Someone grabbed him, dragged him to his feet.

'You all right, Scott?'

Liam shook the voice from his head, ignored the memory, and looked up to see a bedraggled, red-faced Cameron staring at him.

'Sodding ankle,' said Liam. 'You crack on, Dinsdale. Don't fuck your own time up, mate.'

Cameron ignored him. 'Can you stand on it?'

Liam tested it. Pain, then a numbness. 'Leg's dead,' he said, trying again – feeling returning this time. Then he was standing on it, hopping a little, but at least he wasn't on the ground.

'We're over halfway,' said Cameron, still sucking air in like it was about to go up in price.

'I know,' said Liam. 'I can still make it. It's just a sprain.' He pushed Cameron away and started to jog. 'Move it, you twat!' he shouted through gritted teeth. 'I'll see you at the end!'

As Cameron upped a gear and raced off, Liam's first few steps were like someone had replaced his foot with a lump of wood. Gradually, though, it started to work again and soon he was running properly.

He could see the finish now. Each step hurt like hell, but he didn't care. Ignoring the pain, he shook his head, wiped his face, spat and dug deep.

A building zipped by, one Liam knew sat at the one-mile mark. He had only half a mile to go. All he had to do was just keep moving, keep those legs pumping, not stop no matter what his brain and foot was telling him.

More pain. Nausea. Both legs like jelly now. He wanted to throw up, pass out. The urge to stop was overpowering. Liam could feel himself burning up, but the finish line was so close.

Keep going, Liam, just keep going . . .

With a final push, he drew on every ounce of energy and determination he had left.

250 metres . . . 200 metres . . . 150 . . . 100 . . . 50 . . .

Liam crossed the line, his limbs flapping in the air as he lost momentum. But it did nothing to stop him slipping again to the ground and he just sat there, his head spinning, his lungs heaving in and out like a blacksmith's bellows. And his ankle was aching like crazy.

The PTI looked over. 'Nine minutes forty-seven,' he said. 'Well done, Scott. Now get that ankle checked.'

Cameron and Jon came over.

'Pussy,' said Jon.

Liam laughed. 'I'll beat you one day, Renton,' he said, standing up. 'I promise.'

'No fucking chance,' said Jon. 'You're crap. I'm awesome. Deal with it.'

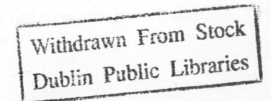

6

It was almost the end of the final term now and the junior soldiers had been bussed up to Scotland to spend seven days and six nights out in the field, using all the skills they'd developed while at the college. It was live firing too, and Liam knew that this was about as real as it was ever going to get without actually having an enemy trying to kill him.

Sitting in a crappy shelter, his shoulders hunched up uselessly against the wind and the rain, he could hardly believe how cold it was. The night before, his water bottle had actually frozen solid. And today – their third – it hadn't seemed like it was going to get any warmer all day.

In some ways he was glad the training was nearly over. It had been tough, frustrating and scary, as well as exciting and exhilarating; there had even been moments when he'd thought about giving up. Then he remembered Matt, binned because of a medical discharge and felt he'd been lucky himself, avoided serious injury, and made it.

Where the hell had the time gone? It didn't seem long since he'd been trying to get used to Army life, which at the start of the course had all seemed so completely and utterly alien. He laughed, remembering how stupid it had seemed being shown not just how to iron a shirt and a pair of trousers with the perfect crease, but even how to take a shower. Did the Army really think people didn't know how to keep their balls clean? Seriously? Apparently so, because they'd had to witness one of the corporals, butt naked, soaping himself up. It was an image he'd tried – unsuccessfully – to forget.

By the end of the first term, Liam had been fitter than he'd ever been in his life – far fitter than he'd ever been when free running – could read a map, strip, clean *and* fire an SA80, do basic first aid and deal with a bullet wound or a broken limb. His teamwork and leadership skills had improved thanks to a stack of outdoor activities like climbing and kayaking.

The second term, though, had upped the military side of things even more and he, like the rest, had made his final choice of which battalion or corps he wanted to join. Sitting in a grey classroom with a group of other junior soldiers and a young officer, Liam had stared at the sheet of paper on the desk in front of him that gave him his options. The officer had laid it on thick how important a decision it was and how it would affect their Army career from that point forwards, but none of it had meant anything to Liam: he had already made his decision. He was joining the Infantry. Nothing else had interested him in the slightest, not least because they all knew that, with the Infantry, there was a greater possibility of them going operational and being sent to Afghanistan. To use his hard-earned skills. To go into action. For real.

Cameron and Jon had chosen the same option.

The final term had been split into three, starting off with all the junior soldiers having to decide if the Army truly was for them or not. If they signed up, then it wasn't for a year or two but for a minimum of four from their eighteenth birthday. For Liam it was a no-brainer; he'd signed up for four years without a second thought. He was turning eighteen within a few days of leaving Harrogate, so those four years were going to start soon. At least now he knew he wouldn't be heading back home in the near future.

Now, though, it was the third night of the final field exercise and the darkness was drawing in with a horrid, soupy gloominess. Liam was having as many conversations with himself to stay motivated as he was with those who'd been put under his command. *His* command. He still couldn't believe it.

Jon was lying on his front, looking out over the lip of the ditch where they'd been placed by one of the other corporals, told to wait for further instructions. That had been twenty-four hours ago. Liam was responsible for one of two light support weapons his section had charge of. Although the LSW was being replaced by a new weapon, it was still used on exercise, particularly with junior soldiers. After all, there was no point in binning a weapon that was still capable of firing its rounds accurately enough to hit a target at up to 1,000 metres. It was essentially the same weapon as the usual SA80 but differed by having a longer free-floating barrel and bipod. Fired in short bursts, it looked more like the kind of rifle that should be belt- not magazine-fed. And that had been its downfall; it just couldn't provide the level of suppressing fire required by soldiers in theatre in the middle of a fire night.

'See anything?'

Jon shook his head. 'Not a thing. Is this going to kick off soon or are we just stuck out here freezing our arses off as some joke by McKenzie and the rest of the happy Officer and NCO club?'

By now Liam and the others were used to Jon's surly attitude. It didn't detract from the fact that he was one of the top junior soldiers in their intake that year. Hard, grumpy, fit: born to be a soldier.

The frustration in Jon's voice was clear and Liam said, 'All I know is all you know, mate. We've been tasked with maintaining this position until the enemy location is identified.'

'That it? Nothing else? Just lie here on our arses until some fucker sends up a flare?'

Liam nodded. He knew that they were all pissed off. An important part of soldiering was understanding that it involved a lot of waiting around and doing nothing, which was exactly what they'd been doing. And that was stressful, because when something did eventually happen, it could be full-on.

'When everything kicks off, our job is to provide covering fire during the attack,' he added.

Liam was impressed with how he sounded. A year ago, none of what he'd just said would have made any sense to him at all. Now, though, he not only understood what the words meant, but could say them with conviction.

'Well, it's bone, Scott, that's what it is,' said one of the other recruits. 'All of it. Completely and utterly bone.'

The other two recruits with Liam were Chris Stevenson and Adam Hurst. It was Chris who'd spoken, a small wiry bloke from Manchester who Liam thought strutted round like a proud cockerel and whose thick

Manchester accent still, after all this time, irritated the living shit out of him.

'Bone?' said Jon, turning on Chris. 'What the fuck are you on about, you knob?'

'Crap,' said Chris. 'Bollocks. Bag of shite. Whatever. It's bone. My brother warned me it would be like this. Can't wait to join him out on tour. Do this for real, right? Slot some Taliban bastards.'

'Best thing you can do is shut the hell up,' said Jon. 'And just focus, right?' He looked over at Liam. 'Did we really have to be stuck with this dickhead?'

Then the sky lit up and all hell broke loose.

Liam saw the flare, a bright orange ball of fire lighting up the sky like a hot sunrise, floating down from above, its fall stalled by the parachute it was attached to.

Gunfire opened up everywhere and the dark evening was blasted apart with bright muzzle flashes that went off like giant exploding fireflies.

Liam's heart was hammering hard. He forced himself to think.

'Stevenson!'

Chris, though, was just staring, mesmerized by the flare as it floated down.

Liam punched him on the arm. 'Covering fire, Stevenson, you fuckwit!' he yelled, kicking Chris hard. 'Fucking well open fire!'

Chris just stared back, his eyes wide. He wasn't doing anything. Just breathing, and cradling his weapon, and grinning stupidly.

'What the hell's wrong with him?' shouted Jon.

'He's frozen!' shouted Liam. 'All that fucking gob on him as well, the twat! Rapid fire! Now!'

Jon and Adam opened up on where Liam had ordered. The sounds and smells and emotions were awesome. It was as exciting as it was terrifying. And now Chris sparked up and was on his weapon too.

Liam saw one of the other sections coming in from the right, advancing on the enemy position, no doubt practising their fire-manoeuvre drills as they went. Watching them, his senses were on full alert. As commander of a fire team, he had to be seriously careful now. Suppressing fire was all about giving cover to those carrying out the attack. And they had to make damned sure that they didn't go spraying the advancing rifle group with live rounds. It was all about providing that covering fire until the last safe moment and no longer.

'Stop!'

Adam and Jon obeyed immediately, easing back on their triggers, their weapons falling silent. Then, as Liam was about to look out to see how the attack was doing, Chris let out a war cry and pulled the trigger.

'Hold your fire, Stevenson!' yelled Liam. 'Hold your fire!'

Chris did nothing of the sort.

'I said stop firing! What the fuck are you doing?'

'You called it too early!' Chris shouted back, and squeezed the trigger again.

'Bloody well hold your fire and that's an order, Stevenson!' shouted Liam, his voice breaking into a scream. 'Now!'

At last Chris did as he was ordered, but he turned immediately on Liam.

'Don't you fucking order me about!' he yelled. 'You sound more like McKenzie than he does! And what are you anyway? Just a junior soldier like me, that's what. You're fuck all, Scott. So shut your mouth and piss off until you know what you're talking about!'

Liam worked hard to stay calm, but it wasn't easy. Chris was getting right in his face, and that accent was making him feel violent.

'What you just did was potentially life-threatening . . .'

Chris pushed Liam in the chest. 'Didn't you hear me? I told you to piss right off!'

'Back off!' ordered Liam, clenching and unclenching his fists. 'Back off and sort your head out, Stevenson!'

Chris did anything but: moving in, and with no

warning at all, he cracked Liam across the cheek with a fist just hard enough to make him yelp.

Liam breathed deep as he saw Jon and Adam close in behind Chris. He held up a hand to get them to stop, not least because he saw blood in Jon's eyes.

'I could have you back-termed for that,' said Liam, now staring at Chris. 'You're a fucking liability, Stevenson. What the hell are you on?'

'And you've got witnesses,' said Jon.

'Two of them,' added Adam. 'And I'd be happy to see this dicksplash gone.'

Chris sneered. 'You wouldn't fucking dare.'

'He doesn't need to,' said a voice from the dark as Corporal McKenzie, ever-watchful, stepped down to join them.

'Bollocks,' said Chris.

'You could say that,' said McKenzie.

But Chris was lucky. When the exercise finally came to an end, and the junior soldiers were bussed back to Harrogate, he got off with the same as Liam had received for his misdemeanour with the SA80 – a fine and a hefty bollocking. He could easily have been back-termed, or even binned completely.

The remainder of Liam's time at Harrogate flew by and it was suddenly graduation day. He'd have put money on his parents not being up in the grandstand at the side of the parade ground with those of the other junior soldiers. A small part of him hoped that they were, if only so that they could see he wasn't going to end up like his dad, but the part that had accepted his parents' complete lack of interest in anything he was doing didn't really care. He'd joined up because he'd decided to go there. All they'd done was sign a piece of paper.

The wind was cold like a blast from an open walk-in freezer, but Liam didn't notice it. He had other things on his mind – mainly not screwing up as the company sergeant major, who was taking the drill parade, barked his orders. Like he'd been marching his whole life, Liam, in formation with the rest of the recruits – Cameron to his right, Jon to his left – wheeled round the edge of the parade ground. The sound of their steps was a steady, mechanical beat that seemed to ricochet off the ground like slow bursts of bullets.

Liam was focused, didn't want to mess this up.

Another order, and he came to a dead stop, turned to face the CSM, snapped to attention.

All Liam could hear was his own breathing, deep and steady. Eyes forward, he sensed someone approaching from his right, and out of the corner of his eye he could see Corporal McKenzie and the CSM walking down the line, checking the recruits. Another officer was with them – a lieutenant colonel, the commanding officer of the college. Strange, Liam thought, how he'd miss Corporal McKenzie after the graduation; his respect for the man had grown throughout the training and he knew he'd never forget him – his hard training, and the serious bollockings.

'Mr Scott,' said the lieutenant colonel, now standing directly in front of Liam, having spent the past few minutes going down the line of recruits at Liam's side.

'Sir!' said Liam, his voice clear and loud.

The lieutenant colonel held out his hand. 'You've reached a major milestone in your career with the British Army. I hope you reach many more. Well done! This is a day to be proud of, so make sure that you are, yes?'

The lieutenant colonel moved on down the line.

A while later, parade was over.

'We nailed it,' said Cameron, turning to Liam. 'Fucking awesome.'

'Fuck knows how,' said Liam. 'I'm knackered.'

Jon joined them. 'Time to go meet the olds, right?' he said. 'Assuming you've actually got parents, Dinsdale.'

'Oh, I've got parents all right,' said Cameron. 'Look.'

As he pointed to the grandstand, they all saw, at the same time, a couple standing apart from the others. The man was clearly uncomfortable, his suit a deep green tweed that didn't quite fit around the shoulders or stomach. The woman was wearing something similar, with a skirt, and the addition of a big, Sunday-morning-at-church hat.

'Is your dad dressed in camo?' asked Liam.

Cameron shook his head. 'He's got one suit and he wears that shooting as much as anywhere else. Yours not here, then?'

Liam shook his head, at the same time realizing he didn't even care. If they'd turned up, he'd have only wondered what they wanted. And, knowing his dad, it would probably have been a loan. 'Come on,' he said, making a move. 'I may as well meet your parents. Got to be better than mine, right?'

Cameron laughed and slapped Liam on the back. 'If you want, I can have them adopt you.'

Liam almost took him seriously.

7

'Show me your war face! Come on, you fuckers – scream!'

Liam was lined up with a group of other soldiers in a field at Catterick Garrison. His graduation from his Phase 1 training at the Army Foundation College was now well behind him, and with the other recruits who had made it this far, he couldn't wait for Phase 2 to start.

He pulled his face into a horror-film snarl and roared. The corporal had, for the past thirty minutes or so, been working at getting Liam and the rest of them to feel aggressive. As yet, for Liam anyway, it wasn't quite working. He had nothing to be pissed at, so he just felt like a tit, screaming his head off and trying to look mean.

Corporal Burns, a man as tall and big as his voice was loud, bellowed once more, and again Liam responded, shouting and yelling like he was about to be a part of the Charge of the Light Brigade.

It was for once a hot day, though Liam fully expected it to turn into another storm of wind and rain. But for now, the air was filled with the smell of hot, sticky tarmac. The sky was empty of everything except an angry sun and the wisps of transatlantic vapour trails from distant aircraft.

Liam screamed again, the corporal giving no indication that he was going to let up on them and give them a break. Liam thought life at Harrogate had been tough, but Catterick made it all pale in comparison. And he had a deep suspicion that it was only going to get much, much worse from here on in. He could deal with it, though. He had to. He wanted to be a soldier more than anything he'd ever wanted in his life before.

Liam was sweating hard, could taste salt on his lips, and they hadn't even been for a run yet that day. The way he was feeling, Harrogate may as well have been a lifetime ago – it had nothing on this, nothing at all.

'To close and engage with the enemy with bayonets fixed?' shouted Corporal Burns, grabbing everyone's attention. 'That's right up fucking close, that is, lads. It's personal.'

Liam knew the corporal had a point. Shooting some-one was in a completely different league to taking it to them with a knife.

'You're not firing at them from a couple of hundred

metres away,' continued the corporal. 'You're not dropping a mortar on a position you can't really see or calling in air support. This is the nasty side of soldiering. The blood and guts side. It works on a psychological level. And can be absolutely fucking devastating.'

Liam didn't disagree. No one did.

'Your aim is to make the enemy shit themselves,' continued the corporal. 'If anyone sees you with a bayonet fitted and you're running at them to shove it into their sternum, then they're going to want to get the hell out, aren't they?'

Corporal Burns gave the recruits a moment or two to think on what he'd just said.

'Think about it, what it involves, right? You're going to be close enough to hug them if you want this to be effective. And you've got to have it in you to take that blade and ram it home, twist the thing in their guts, shred their intestines. Understand?'

'Yes, Corporal!'

In reply Corporal Burns barked out the order, 'Fix bayonets! Remove scabbards!'

Liam was clutching his SA80 tight enough for his knuckles to go white. Following the corporal's instructions, he fixed his bayonet to the weapon and removed the scabbard. The razor-like edge of the bayonet blade glinted in the bright light of the day and

Liam was struck by the awful violence the deadly shard of metal was capable of.

Out in front of them, and about fifty metres away, a number of dummies were strung onto simple wooden frames, weighed down with sandbags to stop them toppling over. Beyond these, further dummies lay fixed to the ground. Liam knew these were the enemy waiting to be charged. And by now the adrenaline had started flowing.

'*On guard!*' ordered the corporal, his voice spitting out like gunfire. He was now walking up and down the line of recruits and working hard to get them even more steamed up. And it was working too, thought Liam.

The corporal leaned in close to Liam and jabbed his finger at him.

'They've just killed your bloody mate! Blown him apart with a grenade. You'd want to kill them too, right?'

'Yes, Corporal!'

'Then show me you want to bloody well kill them, Scott! Come on! Show me that aggression! Fucking well get angry, damn it!'

Liam was raging now. He was so geared up that he almost couldn't wait, could already visualize ramming the bayonet home, ripping through flesh and bone, just killing and killing and fighting and yelling.

Corporal Burns moved down the line, picking on other soldiers, screaming at them. Liam joined in a chant of, 'Kill! Kill! Kill! Kill!'

The word took him over, and if he hadn't been a part of it he would never have believed it was happening. But it was – he was right in the thick of it, and he could feel the effects of it now, his adrenaline burning through him, wiring him to explode.

Liam's throat was sore, his neck straining as he yelled louder and louder. At first he'd felt like a total idiot, screaming out in front of people he'd known for over a year. Then someone had giggled and ended up incurring the wrath of one of the corporals.

'You wouldn't bloody laugh on the battlefield with your guts ripped out, would you?'

That had changed it for everyone. They'd all taken it seriously from that point on. And now they wanted to kick off. And the more Liam thought about it, and the more the aggression of the whole group increased, the more desperate he was to just let rip and tear into the dummies with everything he had inside him.

'Advance!'

On that call, Liam moved forward with the first line of recruits. All he could see was the dummy ahead of him, and all he wanted to do was gut it like a rabbit.

With each step closer the chant of 'Kill! Kill! Kill! Kill!' continued.

'What do you want to do to the enemy? Kill them, that's what! *You want to fucking kill them!*'

With a raging yell that heaved up from his stomach and punched out of his throat, Liam slammed his bayonet hard into the dummy, stabbing into it again and again and again. Blood-red liquid burst from the dummy's gut, spattering the bayonet's deadly steel blade, Liam's own hands, his face.

'Move it, soldier! Move! Stop being weak and keep moving! There's another enemy ahead! Kill them! Do it! Bloody well get a move on!'

Liam yanked his bayonet free, eyeballed the dummy ahead of him lying on the ground, and charged. He was still screaming, and when he got to the dummy he drove his bayonet in with such force it got stuck. More blood-red liquid burst out, not just with the initial stab, but when he eventually managed to pull the blade free. It bubbled up, splashed on him, on the grass, the red of it a horrid slick of gore against the green.

'Fix scabbards!'

But Liam didn't want to fix scabbards – he wanted to keep going, to let the violence and the excitement and the adrenaline take him over completely, to drive him ever onwards, away from his old life and on to everything the training would lead to.

And he, like every other recruit, knew what that meant.

A tour in Afghanistan.

8

'We all know,' said the Army chaplain at the front of the hall, 'that death isn't something anyone really wants to think about.'

Liam knew what vicars were supposed to look like and this one certainly didn't look anything like how he imagined, all weak and grey and old. He was tall, built as well as any of the corporals and sergeants in the room, and about as wet and pathetic as a nice bloody steak. Rumour had it that he was a dab hand in the boxing ring as well.

'But in your line of work, it's a part of what you do. You're in the Army. You can't escape that really, can you? And no matter what precautions we take, through training or body armour or whatever, there's a chance that you, or I, will be killed. And it's time to realize that right now.'

'Never crossed my mind,' said Cameron, leaning over. 'You?'

'It's not an easy thing to come to terms with,' continued the chaplain, 'but if you want to stay sane and do your job well, then you'd better do so from now on in.'

Liam said nothing, just listened.

'Very few come back dead,' said the chaplain, 'but some do – I'm sure you've all seen the repatriations on the telly. And the reality is this . . .' He paused to make sure his words sank in. 'Out of everyone here now, at least one of you is going to die and one will be maimed. Those are the odds. It's sobering, but it's true.'

'Not exactly the happiness guru, is he?' said Cameron.

Liam tried to ignore him as the chaplain was still talking.

'So how many of you in here have a will?'

Liam saw that only a few hands were raised into the air. His wasn't one of them. A will? He'd always seen those as something old people had, not someone like him.

'The rest of you need to have one drawn up pronto,' said the chaplain. 'It's not morbid, it's sensible. It's a good thing. No one wants to be sorting out your stuff when they're also trying to deal with the fact that you're gone. So make it easy on them. You owe it to them, don't you think?'

Liam had never really thought about it like that: his parents not just dealing with his death, but his stuff too. Not that he had much. But the idea of them – particularly his mum – sifting through his belongings choked him a little and he had to force himself to keep with the chaplain and what he was saying.

'And I'd advise all of you to do death letters,' said the chaplain. 'They're quite simple: just a letter from you to your loved ones that only gets delivered if you should be killed.'

The room fell silent. No one spoke, and in the silence Liam allowed the real meaning of what the chaplain had just said to sink in. Not that he'd never thought about the risks involved before, but here and now, that aspect of Army life was being forced on them all. They couldn't avoid it.

'But be careful, OK?' added the chaplain, a faint smile slipping across his face. 'Think about who you send them to. If you've got four girlfriends, drop three of them before you go on tour. Otherwise it just gets complicated.'

A laugh, nervous but welcome none the less, flittered around the room. And while it took its time to settle, Liam thought for a moment about what his own death letter would be like and what he'd write in it. Letters had never been his thing, certainly not ones to his parents.

And despite the fact that, since graduating, he'd at least grown a little closer to his mum, he really had no idea what he'd put in a letter to his parents. Still, he knew the chaplain had a point. If the time came for him to head out on tour – and it most likely would be sooner rather than later – he'd put something down on paper. Perhaps then he'd be able to think of something to say. Now, though, his mind was blank.

A week or so after the chaplain's talk, Liam was with a group in a grey classroom. A young officer was with them. It was a bright day, but the sun was having no effect on the dullness inside.

On the desk in front of him was a sheet of paper – a form to be filled in – and a pen. Back at Harrogate, like the rest of the junior soldiers, Liam had chosen the corps or battalion he had wanted to join. That had been easy: he'd gone, like his mates, for the Infantry. Now, though, it was time to aim for a specific regiment. The list was extensive and Liam realized he wasn't exactly sure which to go for. He knew it was a no-brainer for Jon, who'd made no secret of the fact that he'd turned up at Harrogate with the sole aim of eventually becoming a Para like his dad. As for himself, however, he had no particular reason, family connection or otherwise, to choose any specific regiment, be it the Mercian or the Grenadiers.

But he had to make a choice, right here, right now.

The officer was tall, athletic and looked barely older than Liam or anyone else in the room. But when he spoke, his voice had the measured clarity of someone who'd walked a university degree and thoroughly enjoyed everything that the Royal Military Academy at Sandhurst – the British Army's officer training college – could throw at him.

'Of all those who started at Harrogate with you,' he said, 'only two thirds now remain. That in itself is one hell of an achievement.'

It was a sobering figure – Liam had never really thought about the number of junior soldiers who'd had to drop out. He was secretly proud to still be there and to have survived.

'What you need to understand, lads,' continued the officer, 'is that once you decide, that's it, there's no changing your minds, and you will go where your regiment goes. And regardless of what you choose, it will, almost certainly, involve a tour of Afghanistan. That is a fact, and an unavoidable one at that.'

There was silence after those words. Liam was acutely aware that what he did with the pen in his hand would radically alter his whole life. Even, possibly, end it. And that was the crux of it all, wasn't it? he thought. This wasn't just a case of running around a forest and playing soldiers any more. With the stroke of a pen he was saying that he was happy and willing to be sent into harm's way, into a war zone. A place where people, blokes like him, got injured, got killed.

Liam remembered what the chaplain had said about the death letters and the odds being that at least one of them would be killed. Would it be him? Would it be Cameron? He didn't want to think about it, but figured that at that moment he probably wasn't the only one mulling that thought over.

'You also need to understand,' continued the officer, 'that although you are given a choice of which regiment you want to join, the Army has the final say. Period. You have only a one-in-five chance of getting the battalion you choose. And even then, I wouldn't put money on it.'

Liam briefly wondered what, then, the point was of asking them to choose in the first place. Jon getting into the Paras was down to more than just deciding to join. He'd have to prove himself on a completely new level just to make it through. As for him and Cameron, he didn't want to think about the possibility of them being in different battalions. It was good to have a mate by your side, and Liam knew Cameron was someone he could depend on when things got down and dirty. He tuned back into what the officer at the front of the room was saying.

'For your information, and as a heads up, 2 Rifles is not only lowest on numbers but will be preparing for its next tour of Afghanistan when you finish here. The Army can't send a battalion out that's low on numbers. Understand?'

Everyone in the room nodded. Yeah, thought Liam, we all understand. It wasn't like the message was hidden, was it?

'That's the reality, lads,' continued the officer. 'When the order comes to go, that's what you do, you go. And know this also: the Army will always come first. Always. Your life, and that of your family, comes second. That's just the way it is.'

The officer fell silent. Liam took his pen and started writing.

9

'May as well have a big fucking spotlight on us,' said Cameron, as experienced soldiers from 2 Rifles, the regiment both he and Cameron had chosen – Jon, as he had wished, had got into the Paras and was out of their lives now – funnelled into the room they were sitting in. 'I feel like a right tit.'

Phase 2 training was over and Liam was no longer a junior soldier but a fully signed-up member of the British Army. A soldier. Deep down, though, he was aware that right now, in this room, that meant absolutely sod all.

The soldiers he was now surrounded by were all veterans of recent combat operations in Iraq and Afghanistan. Though some were barely older than himself, they still looked aged by what they'd experienced, what they'd seen. Occasionally one would walk in built like a rugby player, with arms as thick as tree trunks, but most were wiry, like athletes; runners, rather than gym rats. Liam sensed an air of confidence about them, not just in how they walked, but in the way they handled themselves, the way they talked to each other.

As for him, at that moment, it all seemed astonishingly unreal. He'd completed his basic training and was now only six months away from his first tour of duty in Afghanistan. With the room now full, an officer stood up at the front and everyone fell quiet.

'First, for those new to 2 Rifles, welcome,' he said, his voice clear and direct. 'My name is Major Edwards. We have less than six months to prepare for combat in Afghanistan. And it's my job, and that of every other commissioned and non-commissioned officer in this room, to make sure that is exactly what we do.'

Major Edwards looked like a walking advert for Sandhurst, thought Liam. Tall and upright, he spoke not just with confidence but a certainty that what he said would happen, and happen now, no questions asked.

For the next few minutes, the major outlined what the training would involve, and Liam's stomach refused to stop twisting itself tighter and tighter, not just with nerves, but with excitement.

'Mark my words, gentlemen,' Major Edwards concluded forcefully, 'we *will* be prepared. None of you will go to Afghanistan unable to implement your training above and beyond the best of your ability. You will be ready.'

The following day, Liam was stripping an SA80, a task he'd grown used to through his Phase 1 and 2 training. He'd laid everything, from the retaining spring to the barrel, out on a plastic sheet on the floor. It had taken him longer than usual to get to this point, but he ignored the irritation and got on with the job in hand.

A sergeant by the name of Reynolds came over. He had a ratty look to his face; indeed, his whole body seemed built for wriggling through small spaces. And his eyes never seemed to blink.

'You're just tickling them,' he said, clearly irritated by how long it was taking some of them, including Liam and Cameron, to clean their weapons. 'They're not bloody pets! Get some oil on those rags and get them cleaned!'

Liam did as the sergeant had said and worked from one end of the sheet to the other, cleaning each part meticulously. But, as he reassembled the weapon, the barrel slipped out of his hand.

Liam heard laughter. Not daring to look, and horribly aware now that he was being watched, his clumsiness seemed to take over as he picked up the barrel, and immediately the rest of the weapon fell apart.

Liam swore out loud, picked up the barrel to fix it in place, and noticed that the laughter had stopped dead. Looking up, he saw that another soldier was staring over at him, an SA80 – already stripped, cleaned and re-assembled – cradled casually in his hands. He was standing alone, but it seemed not so much out of choice but because those around him didn't want to get too close, like they were either afraid of him, or in awe, or perhaps a bit of both.

Sunlight now in his eyes, Liam could only make out the figure's silhouette. Then he heard footsteps and realized that the soldier was making his way slowly towards him.

His steps were slow, purposeful, and his eyes were clearly focused on Liam as he drew closer. There was a look of surprise on his face.

Liam recognized him at once and his heart sank.

'Mike . . .'

'Hello, Liam.'

Liam noticed other soldiers watching. They reminded him of vultures circling a killing.

'It's been a long time.'

Liam nodded, his mouth dry. Mike Hacker? Here? What the hell was going on? It couldn't be possible! Not only that, it wasn't bloody fair – not now, not with everything going so well!

'Funny how we should meet like this, isn't it?' said Mike, his voice calm, confident. 'What are the odds, eh?'

Liam didn't like Mike's serrated tone of voice.

'Look, I'm sorry . . .' he said, but Mike held up a hand.

'We all are,' he said, each word measured, 'but we both know that means fuck all, right?'

Liam didn't respond, had no idea how to, was completely unprepared. For a moment, they just stared at each other, then Mike turned away.

Liam watched as the other man walked off and disappeared from view, soldiers folding in behind him, all of them looking at Liam, their eyes clearly questioning what they'd just witnessed.

Cameron came over, ever-alert to trouble around his mate. 'Who the fuck was that, Scott?'

Liam was in shock and had to work hard to stop himself once again fumbling as he reassembled his weapon. When it was finally together, he stood up.

'I didn't join the Army just because I wanted to,' he said slowly. 'I joined to escape, get away.'

'So fucking what?' said Cameron. 'We all did, right? Isn't that what the Army's all about? Isn't that why most of us join up in the first place?'

Liam shook his head. His past was rushing at him now, demanding attention.

'Back home, I was out with some mates . . .' He paused, remembered, stumbled over his words. 'We were messing around, you know? Doing a bit of free running, shit like that.'

Cameron screwed up his face. 'You mean that jumping and swinging all over the place like a monkey?' he said. 'Are you fucking serious?'

Liam nodded. 'I was pretty good at it and the others followed me. But . . .' He didn't want to say any more. It was too painful. And that nightmare, the figure at the end of his bed . . . he didn't want that coming back. Not now.

'But what?' Cameron asked. 'What happened?'

Liam paused, took a breath, composed himself. 'There was . . . an accident,' he said haltingly. 'My best mate, Dan, was killed. Fell off a roof. Died on the way to hospital. I was with him in the ambulance.'

Cameron looked serious and for a moment said nothing.

'So what's that got to do with what just happened?'

Liam stared back at where Mike had gone.

'Last time I saw him was at the funeral,' he said, working hard to keep his voice steady. 'I knew he was in the forces, but seriously? What are the odds of us being in the same bloody regiment?'

'So who is he?'

Liam released a deep sigh. 'Dan's older brother.'

10

Liam stared at the pictures on the screen. He knew what they were, they all did: Improvised Explosive Devices. IEDs. And the news seemed to be increasingly filled with stories about soldiers being smashed to pieces by them.

The pictures were labelled as victim-operated, suicide, suicide vehicle-borne, and remote control. Sergeant Reynolds, a veteran of Afghanistan and Iraq and God knows where else, was at the front of the class, his face as pissed off and mean as ever.

'2 Rifles is an Infantry regiment,' he said, clearly proud of the fact. 'You will fight on your feet, engaging with the enemy face-to-face.' He jabbed a calloused finger at the screen like he was about to ask it out for a fight. 'And these are the types of IED you're going to face.'

He paused to stare at each of the soldiers in the room in turn, then spoke again.

'This is what we do, right? And because of it, you're going to be more exposed to the threat of IEDs than all those soldiers who get to mooch around in armoured vehicles all day like they're out on safari.'

Liam stared at the pictures. One IED was just a clay jug. It looked harmless, but he knew it could probably blow his legs off, if not rip him to shreds and turn him into pink mist.

Sergeant Reynolds continued. 'Question: how many soldiers in Afghanistan have been killed by IEDs since 2006?'

The room was silent. Liam hadn't a clue what the answer was.

'Too fucking many,' said the sergeant, as though he'd fully expected no one to get the answer. 'With hundreds more seriously injured. For every British soldier killed on the battlefield, four are being seriously injured. And these bastard things are to blame, more than anything else.'

He pointed again at the screen.

'These things scare the shit out of me. I don't mind admitting it. And they should do the same to you. If they don't, then fuck off out of 2 Rifles and do something else. I don't want you here and I sure as hell don't want to be fighting alongside you in a few months' time. Because that's exactly what we're going to be doing.'

Liam found it almost impossible to believe that Sergeant Reynolds was scared of anything at all. If he was, it made the seriousness of what he was saying somehow even more acute.

'Some of these devices can even be set off by a torch beam,' continued the sergeant. 'You go and do a sweep of a room, click your torch on and that's it, *boom*. Game over.'

Liam was liking this session less and less. It was as though Sergeant Reynolds wanted to scare them. But then he probably did, didn't he? And Liam wanted to make sure every word he heard didn't just sink into his brain, but really took root. Listening today could save his life – and those of his mates – in the future.

'And whether I like you or not,' said the sergeant, yanking Liam from his thoughts, 'and believe me, I probably won't, I'm going to do my best to make sure that you lot have enough information in your thick skulls to ensure that you don't add to those numbers. Understand?'

Soon after the haunting session on IEDs, out on patrol, Liam's mind was still bouncing between worrying about Mike, and worrying about being blown up. He still wasn't sure which was worse.

A voice came from behind, breaking him away from his thoughts.

'Lads, who's covering tail-end Charlie?'

The patrol stopped dead.

It was Major Edwards and he was living up to his reputation for being all about the detail.

'Me, sir,' said a soldier called Dave Woods. Liam knew him about as well as he knew anyone else in the company: not at all. His name was apt, though: he was tall and gangly like a sapling, and camo'd up, he looked like a rubbish tree.

The major walked over. When he next spoke his voice was quiet, serious.

'Woods, you're supposed to be checking all around,' he said, leaning in, his voice growing louder, 'not just glancing left and right, swinging your weapon around like a bloody dog's lead!'

Dave said nothing, looked like his voice had got stuck in his throat, and the major jabbed a pointed finger at the ground.

'All this is unchecked ground. For all you know, there could be an IED you've missed because of being so slack! Then what? Some poor sod comes up behind and they end up dead because you didn't do your bloody job properly! Is that what you want, soldier? To have their eyeballs bounce off your back as they're blown to Kingdom Come?'

Even though Liam knew he wasn't the one being

bollocked, the major's words seemed to hit him just as hard as they did Woods.

'That's why we're doing this,' the major continued, his eyes not leaving Dave for a second. 'To make sure you get it right here and don't go screwing this up in theatre, got it?'

'Sir.'

Liam watched as the major left Woods swearing to himself. Walking over to have a quick word with one of the two soldiers out front, the one tasked as section commander, Major Edwards then waved them all on.

A few days later, and after more foot patrol practice, live firing, and compound search training, Liam was once again on patrol in the rain. He was cold, wet and bored.

'Not like in the movies, is it?'

Liam was with Dave, who spoke with a Geordie accent that made him sound as though no matter what he was doing, he was enjoying it. Even if he wasn't. Living on rations in a shelter that had failed miserably, and only ever getting a maximum of four hours' sleep, they were both exhausted.

'How do you mean?' asked Liam, his hands icy cold as they held his SA80.

'Well, you never see this, do you?' said Dave, looking about them and kicking his foot in a puddle. 'Two blokes standing in the rain, bored to death, then going home having done nothing? Aren't we supposed to be abseiling out of helicopters and shit like that?'

Standing in the rain wasn't really in any of the Army's promotional literature either, thought Liam with a laugh. But he knew enough to realize that soldiering was as much about routine tasks as it was explosive fire-fights. And everything had to be done correctly; if you got the little things wrong, like washing your bollocks, then who was to say you wouldn't screw up when the bullets were flying?

'You've got us confused with *Black Hawk Down*,' he said, checking his watch. 'Anyway, we've only got a few hours left till we get picked up. Then we're doing compound search training, I think. Should be better than this.'

'Couldn't be much worse, right?'

'Huh, wait till we get out to Afghanistan,' Liam retorted.

'Yeah,' said Cameron, who had stepped up to join them. 'And you know, most of me can't wait to get the fuck out there, to do what we've been training for; I want to get on with it, prove I won't brick it when it gets real!'

'Don't you get all shaky,' said Liam. 'Afghanistan won't be half as much fun if you're not out there with me enjoying all that death-at-every-corner stuff.'

'And we'll find out just how much fun when we're back from leave, won't we?' said Cameron.

Liam raised an eyebrow. 'We don't head out for a couple of months.'

'I'm not talking about Afghanistan,' said Cameron. 'I'm talking about Norfolk.'

11

A couple of weeks later, with a period of leave coming and going so quickly that Liam could hardly remember what he'd done with it – though he and Cameron had hit the pubs pretty hard, and copped off with a girl or two who he could only vaguely remember – he was sitting next to Cameron on another Army coach. This time they were bound for a multi-million-pound training area in Norfolk where a small part of Afghanistan had been brought to the English country-side.

'Apparently it's full-on realistic,' said Cameron, his eyes closed, head back against the seat. 'It's even been populated with Afghan nationals, so it's the closest we'll get to being in Afghanistan without actually being right there in the middle of all that dust and heat.'

'It's just like the major said,' said Liam with a smile. 'You've done primary school, now you're at secondary school. But when you get to Afghanistan, you'll be at the university of hard knocks.'

'You've got to love the man's use of clichés,' said Cameron. 'You reckon they get presented with a book of them to use when they graduate from Sandhurst?'

The coach slowed and eased off the main road, turning down a track almost completely hidden by trees. It was like travelling down a dark green tunnel.

'Reckon we're nearly there,' said Liam, looking down the aisle of the coach.

'Thank fuck for that,' said Cameron. 'My arse is numb from the journey and I couldn't half do with a shit.'

The compound itself was a snapshot of what Liam had seen of Afghanistan in pictures, on the news, and on the films they'd seen during training. Surrounded by high walls, he and the rest of the section were soon walking down an authentic Afghan village street. That he was in Norfolk doing it seemed bizarre in the extreme, as though the Army had somehow airlifted the place from one country to another in secret. People were milling around in traditional Afghan clothes, speaking in a mix of Pashto – the most common Afghan language – and English. An old two-wheeled cart was lying at the side of the road. Further on was a marketplace with someone selling vegetables; someone else had a small butcher's stall, then there was a table with someone selling what looked like vintage bottles of soda.

Well-armed, they carried between them two light machine guns, one Sharpshooter rifle, and five SA80s, two of which were fitted out with the UGL 40mm under-slung grenade launchers – Liam was carrying an LMG which, firing at a rate of 700–1,000rpm, was an absolute beast. And Liam had to admit that having it in his hands made him feel pretty bloody good, if not invincible. Walking down such a street and carrying a weapon like the LMG, despite the whole scene itself being fake, was as surreal and as frightening as it was exciting. Liam was working hard to keep the smile off his face, to stay in character. But it wasn't easy when, even though he knew why they were there and what they were being trained to do, he felt cool.

One of the Afghans ran over and touched Liam's weapon. Surprised, Liam jerked it away, not sure if that was the correct response or not, and kept on walking. Further on, the stallholders called out to them with 'Salaam alaikum' and invites to check out their stalls, to wander over and have a look, try before you buy.

After a while, Liam began to relax into working a foot patrol through an Afghanistan village. Following the lead of some of the other more experienced soldiers, he chatted to the locals, at the same time as keeping eyes on everything that was happening around him. He spotted Mike, but they didn't make eye contact. Since that first meeting, he'd been expecting to run into him at every turn, but the opposite had been true; the major was keeping them all so busy that there was no time for anything but training. And, by luck or good fortune, Liam had not yet had to work alongside Mike. And because of that, though he was still concerned that there was still some serious shit between them that would have to be sorted some time, the fact that Dan's brother was here no longer really bothered him. He was focused now on getting on with what he was there for, why he'd signed up in the first place: to be a soldier, and a good one at that.

It was then, when Liam was completely absorbed in his role, chatting to a local and trying his level best to make him understand that he really wasn't interested in buying a packet of batteries, that an explosion smashed the moment into pieces like a bunk-buster missile.

The peace shattered now, bits of it still rolling around in the air, and the dust continued to swirl as the once-calm street scene descended into utter chaos.

Liam, caught off-guard, his ears ringing with the rip of the explosion, was momentarily disorientated and confused. He'd not expected the explosion. None of them had.

On the ground he spotted a man with a leg missing. Blood was pouring from a mangled stump and beside him was a woman in a burka holding the rest of his leg. She was wailing – and the man was screaming his lungs out.

A hand grabbed Liam's shoulder, whipped him round. 'Scott! Wake up and respond! Come on! Start sparking, for fucksake!' It was Sergeant Reynolds. And Liam could see that the devil was in his eyes. 'We've got four casualties and eyes on possible Taliban!' continued Reynolds. 'Think like a soldier! Move it!'

Liam came to life in a moment as adrenaline poured into him. Everything came into focus as his senses rammed him full of information from what was happening all around.

'Yes, Sergeant!'

Sergeant Reynolds pointed at a soldier lying on the floor, debris covering his head. Liam saw that his chest was a mess of blood and ripped clothing, and for a split second, his eyes told him the wound was real: the blood and the gore were seriously effective and Liam knew that the guys who made up the fake wounds could easily cut it on any good Hollywood horror movie. And the soldier was putting on a performance good enough for the Old Vic, screaming and yelling like he'd had his ribcage ripped out as he threw the fragments of rubble off his face.

'Get your arse over there and evac that casualty now!'

Liam, with three other soldiers who'd joined with him from Harrogate and Catterick, was at the casualty's side in seconds. The casualty grabbed him and screamed at him, covering him in spit, then slapped him across the face with a hand slick with blood. As Liam steadied himself from the blow, the casualty lashed out again, this time at one of the other soldiers. Then he turned back to Liam.

'Bring back memories, Scott?'

'Mike . . . ?'

Liam knew he should've called Mike by his surname, Hacker, but the fact that he'd known him in civilian life had made it difficult not to use his Christian name. And seeing him covered in blood hit Liam like a runaway train. The similarities between Mike and his brother, Dan, were striking. And just for a second, Liam was no longer dealing with a casualty on a foot patrol – he was back at the accident, back at Dan's side as they slammed him into the rear of the ambulance and raced him through the streets and the last few heartbeats he had left.

Liam jerked forward and realized that Mike had him

round the neck. He was screaming at him, shaking him like a rabbit in the jaws of a fox.

'He's fucking going for it, this one, eh?' said a soldier called Miller, reaching over to stop Mike from strangling Liam. 'You'd think he wants you dead, hey, Scott?'

Mike back-handed Miller and sent him sprawling too. Liam saw the soldier snarl and hurl himself back at Mike to restrain him.

'Calm the fuck down!'

Sergeant Reynolds joined in, shouting, 'Bloody well sort him out!' He was up close to watch how they all reacted. 'He's panicking. He's been wounded. He probably thinks you're the Taliban come to take his flamin' nuts off! Get him calm, lads. If you can't deal with this, what sodding use are you to me when the shit's really coming down? Use your training!'

Liam could hardly breathe. Like all the soldiers around him, he'd run through scenarios like this before, dealt with injuries in the battlefield. But his experience was little more than classroom stuff, pretend. He knew that some of them had probably done this for real. And it was showing too, with all the experienced guys reacting properly to the situation in front of them. He needed to get a grip, take control.

The voice drilled into Liam's head again as the sergeant yelled at him to stop dancing with the casualty and get the situation under control. Then Mike relaxed his hold, only to come at Liam again; this time Liam was quick enough to dodge being cracked in the skull and managed to secure Mike's arm to the ground.

'You!' shouted Liam, looking over at Miller, who still looked pissed at Mike for what he'd just done. 'Grab his arm and start talking to him! Tell him it'll be all right, that everything's fine!'

Miller didn't look convinced. 'That fucker chinned me,' he spat back.

'Just do it, Miller!' hissed Liam. 'It's what we have to do, remember? Keep talking to them, keep them calm, and keep their mind off what's happened. Now do it!'

The soldier, hesitant at first, started to do exactly as Liam had said. Liam then looked at the other two soldiers, their names escaping him at that moment. 'We'll hold him down, you two check his wounds and hit him with some morphine to calm him down!'

Mike spat blood into Liam's face. 'Having fun, Liam? Is this what it was like with Dan? His blood all over you as he lay there dying because of you being such a fuckhead?'

Liam ignored Mike and focused on being a soldier.

In a few moments, after quickly checking Mike over, Miller and the other soldiers had dealt with the wound on his chest – a pressure dressing – then mimicked giving him a hit of morphine; soon they were carrying him out of the street on a makeshift stretcher.

The whole thing was over in minutes. From a quiet street scene to absolute chaos and back to calm again. The rush was something else and Liam could see that his hands were shaking with the mix of excitement, fear and adrenaline.

'You all right, Scott?' Cameron was at Liam's side. His kit was covered in blood.

Liam wasn't sure. What he'd just experienced wasn't simply a case of role-play. 'That was pretty realistic,' he said at last. 'I'm still shaking.'

'They use real amputees, fake body parts, proper horror-movie make-up,' said Cameron. 'Worked a treat, didn't it?'

'You could say that,' Liam replied, still trembling a little.

'Yours was really going for it, wasn't he?' said Cameron. 'Proper Oscar-winning stuff. Almost looked personal!'

Liam nodded, then said, 'It was Mike. The bastard went for me like we were in a bar brawl.'

'Fucksake! Did Sergeant Reynolds see it?'

Liam noticed a steeliness in Cameron's look that almost knocked him back.

'Mike didn't just get me,' he said, almost worried about what Cameron was gunning for. 'Had a go at Miller too.'

'That bastard—'

Liam cut Cameron off. 'Mate, it's not worth it.'

'Bollocks it is,' said Cameron, and made to walk over to one of the corporals.

Liam grabbed him. 'Seriously, Dinsdale,' he said, 'Don't. You'll only make it worse.'

'Will I?' said Cameron. 'He's with us in Afghan, Scott. You thought about that?'

Yes, Liam thought, *it's pretty much all I've been thinking about. But there's fuck all I can do about it.*

12

Back at barracks, Liam joined the end of a long queue at the end of which was a photographer snapping a shot of a squaddie. Judging by the awkward look on the man's face, Liam could tell he felt like a complete idiot. He was doing his level best to make sure that the shot was of his best side, which from where Liam was standing was a tough choice – both sides were covered in acne. Like the squaddie, and every other soldier in the queue, Liam was holding a sheet of paper in his hand. On it was written his name, rank, number and regiment.

An officer Liam had never seen before headed towards them. 'Right,' he called out, his voice clear and precise, 'for those of you who've just turned up, the whole point of this is, if there's a hoo-hah in theatre and we need to get a picture of you, for any reason whatsoever, and the clerk on duty doesn't know who you are, we can go through the photograph files and find you nice and easy. That's all there is to it. Happy with that? Good.'

Liam shuffled forwards. He'd never before heard someone refer to anything as a 'hoo-hah'. It didn't seem to quite fit with what the officer was describing – a live firefight or an explosion. But then he'd noticed this more and more during his time in the Army, and particularly since joining 2 Rifles. A sort of blasé attitude to the shit hitting the fan.

He heard a cough and turned to find Mike standing directly behind him. A few other soldiers were nearby, and at the sight of Mike they moved back. At first it reminded Liam of kids in a playground when the bully walks past. But then he realized it was something else. The others were in awe of Mike, like he was some kind of hero to them, a soldier to look up to. And maybe he was, thought Liam, but that didn't alter the fact that he was also a full-on walking tosser.

'You know what these are, right?' said Mike. 'Death photos. Only ever used when someone's killed and we need to identify them.'

'What about the voluntary DNA samples?'

Both he and Cameron had decided to follow the advice they'd all been given and provide a voluntary DNA sample. It was nothing more than a swab from inside his cheek, but the point of it was clear: if something bad happened, and their bodies were in too poor a state to be easily identified, DNA was the only way certainty could be guaranteed.

'You know the odds are some of us won't be coming back, don't you?' said Mike.

'Risk is part of the job,' Liam replied, wishing he would just sod off and leave him alone.

'So you're happy with the fact that you might get killed?'

Mike's face was too close now and Liam could smell cigarette smoke on his breath. He leaned away, but Mike was pushing him, getting in his face, and he'd had enough. He couldn't hold it in any longer.

'What's your problem, Mike? If this is about Dan . . .'

The queue shuffled forward. Liam wanted to get away from Mike, and fast, but he still had his photo to do before he could make a break.

Mike smiled coldly, rested a hand on Liam's shoulder and said softly, 'Afghanistan's a dangerous place, Liam. More dangerous than that stupid factory roof my brother followed you up on to.' His eyes hardened. 'You understand what I'm saying?'

And with that, Mike turned round and walked off, leaving Liam with his sheet of paper and enough to make him think that when he got to Afghanistan it wouldn't just be the Taliban he was going to have to worry about. Mike was gunning for him and that made Liam's gut twist.

'Oi, Scott – what do you think?'

Liam looked over at Cameron, who was wearing a Multi Terrain Pattern helmet perched on top of his head. Photos done, they were now both standing in a warehouse filled with countless brown boxes, all of which were being quickly unpacked and their contents distributed to a slowly moving line of soldiers. Everyone was there, from Major Edwards down. The battalion was getting kitted out for its tour.

'You look like a dick,' said Liam. 'And I mean that literally as well as the other way.'

'You mean figuratively,' said Cameron.

'Yeah, that.'

Cameron removed his helmet, slipped it into a large bag, then tried to pull on a pair of tough-looking gloves. 'Not every day you get to just walk into a shop and take loads of free stuff, is it?' he said, looking at the gloves. 'Wrong size. Typical. I'll have to see if I can get them changed.'

Liam glanced over at the pile of stuff in front of him. Everything was provided, from socks to battle pack to Kevlar plates, all of it new, clean, and wrapped in individual cellophane packets. The whole lot together weighed an absolute ton and Liam knew they'd be picking up their weapons later too.

'Not so sure about these Jesus sandals,' said Cameron, walking over, half carrying, half dragging his bag of kit. 'Looking like a twat isn't why I joined up.'

'At least you won't cut your feet to shreds if you're in the shower and there's an enemy contact,' said Liam, remembering what they'd been told about why the sandals were provided.

'Doubt I'd be too fussed about my feet if the shit kicked off when I was bollock naked in the shower,' said Cameron. 'Reckon I'd be more worried about engaging the enemy with my dick hanging out!'

Laughing, they picked up the rest of their kit, then headed back out of the warehouse, their bags on their shoulders, then on to their quarters.

'One final inspection by Major Edwards, then it's our last leave before we fly out,' said Cameron. 'Lock and load, right?'

Liam noticed that, for once, despite the jokes, his mate didn't sound so confident. He wasn't alone.

A few hours later, Liam joined the rest of 2 Rifles outside the barracks, all of them dressed in their civvies. Major Edwards was standing in front of them to give them a final nod before they went on their last leave before heading off to Afghanistan.

Liam was excited and nervous – he half wished they didn't have to take any leave at all and could just get on a plane and into theatre. He'd never been good at waiting around. But a few days out on the piss would do them no harm – a taste of normality before the immensity of what was ahead.

'First of all,' said the major, 'well done on what you've achieved so far. We're ninety per cent of the way there, so don't slacken off. Those skills you've been working on so hard, we're going to keep working on them. That way, I know I can be confident in you and what we are all there to do.'

He paused for a breath.

'And last of all, before you head off on leave, remember this: keep your fists in your pockets. Anyone gives you grief, just walk away, stay out of trouble and come back here ready for the job you're all trained for. We don't need any dramas, understand? Now, off you go. And enjoy.'

A few days later, Liam was on a transport plane, an eight-hour one-way flight to Camp Bastion. Behind him, the seemingly endless rain of England and months of training. Ahead, the heat of the desert, and the war he was now a part of.

His tour was beginning.

13

The moon was high and clear, and the light from it gave the world around a sort of weak orange glow as the plane came in to Camp Bastion.

Like most other air traffic, they'd landed at night to reduce the risk of attack; the plane's internal lights were shut off as they made their approach to make them harder to spot by any Taliban feeling trigger-happy with an RPG. It was nothing like being on a commercial airliner and Liam had done his best to stay and look calm, as though what they were doing was something he did every day, had done a dozen times before. But he'd still felt nervous as hell when they swung round to make their approach to land, convinced they were about to be blown out of the sky by a well-aimed RPG and scattered all over the desert in a billion tiny pieces of flesh and metal.

Walking away from the plane that had brought him

and the rest of 2 Rifles on his first-ever tour, relieved to be on firm ground, Liam had caught sight of the huge earth-filled bombproof bags that surrounded the camp and had given it its name – a *bastion*. The place truly was a fortress, and one that Liam was more than aware was under constant threat of attack, both from the outside, and from those trying to get in past the guards to blow themselves up and grab a fast track to paradise.

Camp Bastion was a world away from anything Liam had ever experienced in his life before. It was nothing like when he and Cameron had turned up to join 2 Rifles – more like walking into a settlement on Mars. Dust was everywhere, kicked up by passing traffic, covering Liam's clothing within moments, and he could taste it in the back of his throat and up his nose. He felt parched almost immediately and was glad of the bottles of water that had been thrust into their hands.

Moving away from the runway, he soon realized that going anywhere in the camp at night would be nigh on impossible without a torch. There were no pavements, no street lights. Hardly any light seemed to manage to escape from the tents or other structures they passed as they snaked through the camp; all were hidden behind huge walls of sandbags to protect them from any ordnance landing inside the camp's perimeter. Liam knew that it had happened, if not regularly, certainly frequently; and he was glad to see that even here they were given some protection.

Since the start of the war, Camp Bastion had grown to four times its original size, housing thousands of Coalition troops. And with over six hundred flights each day, it was as busy as most civilian airports back in the UK. The size of it was not lost on Liam as he was taken to where he would be bedding down. They would stay here for the next five nights while they acclimatized to life in Afghanistan. It was a huge canvas tent which could sleep up to thirty-two soldiers on bunk beds. Other accommodation was provided – metal pods with hard roofs – but these, Liam knew, were used only by VIPs. He wasn't so sure they were any better off, though; the beds weren't the best he'd slept on, but neither were they the worst. And as for having to live under a tin lid, he'd take his chances with canvas. VIP or not, it didn't strike him as any kind of luxury, not with Afghanistan capable of hitting a temperature of 55°C in the summer, then freezing in the winter.

The next day he got a better view of the camp, and was even more awed by the place than when they'd landed. He knew the figures – that it could easily house between 20,000 and 30,000 troops and associated staff at any one time – but the sheer scale of it was almost impossible to comprehend. It was a desert-locked city built by the military, and though it may have been temporary, Liam couldn't for the life of him see how such a place could ever just disappear again and leave blank Afghan desert.

What seemed like thousands of huge tents and other part-canvas, part-steel structures vied for space with other freight containers that Liam had really only ever seen before on lorries or ships, or rusting away in some of the rundown factory sites and derelicts that he'd explored as a kid. Dogs were everywhere, patrolling and sniffing for drugs and explosives, as well as standing guard at checkpoints.

As he would only be in Camp Bastion for five days, Liam knew that his time there would be seriously busy, his hours crammed with training and fitness. And for that he was grateful. Not just because he wanted to be as switched on and prepared for what he was to face as possible, but also because it didn't look like the kind of place he wanted to have to stay around for too long, anyway. Despite the vast number of cafés, restaurants and gyms that were dotted around the enormous camp, Liam wanted to be where the action was. He couldn't wait to go on patrol.

Chinook helicopters, or *cows* as he'd heard many of the experienced soldiers in 2 Rifles call them, seemed to fill the air, constantly ferrying equipment and troops in and out of the camp, filling the air with an everlasting and choking fog of orange dust. Liam had no doubt that some of them were carrying either injured soldiers back to the camp hospital, or surgeons out to a casualty to start working on saving lives as quickly as they could. As well as the Chinooks, Apache choppers buzzed around in formation, sweeping across the camp like great angry wasps.

Liam saw Warrior troop carriers, Jackals, the Foxhound – the replacement for the Land Rover Snatch – and plenty of other vehicles he'd only really ever seen before on film or in pictures. Land Rovers were still used inside the camp and there were motorbikes too, two-wheeled and quads. The speed limit of 24kph (15mph) didn't seem to make that much difference whenever the huge and imposing Mastiff drove by. A six-wheel drive, heavily armoured vehicle, it looked like it had been designed with the sole purpose of scaring the hell out of anyone in its way. The ground shook as it rolled by, almost as though it, too, was afraid.

'So, Dinsdale, who's briefing us?'

Liam had experienced his first night's sleep on Afghanistan's soil but was still tired. He also knew that from now on sleep was going to be a luxury and he'd have to grab what shuteye he could whenever he got the chance.

He was sitting beside Cameron, and with the rest of 2 Rifles, in a huge temporary hall built from steel supports with canvas walls. Outside, a bright sun was burning the day with the heat of an open furnace door. Dust filled the air, kicked up by the hundreds of vehicles passing into and out of the camp. The air was dry as tinder, and every time Liam breathed in, he could taste not just the desert, but the heat, the vehicles, the kitchens, even the latrines. The water did something to alleviate it, quenching his thirst, but it didn't take away the taste.

Cameron was yawning like he was attempting to suck in a basketball.

Liam nudged him to get an answer to his question. 'Wake up, Dinsdale, you dick,' he said.

'The largest Coalition force over here,' drawled Cameron in response, as he rubbed his eyes. 'The United States Marine Corps. *Ooh-rah!*'

Recognizing Cameron's attempt at the battle cry of the corps, Liam laughed.

Cameron pointed at a soldier at the front of the gathering crowd and Liam glanced over at the US Marine Corp sergeant. His chest looked unfeasibly large, like he'd been born doing bench-presses. Liam had heard that weight-training and body-building was how a huge number of soldiers based at Camp Bastion spent their time, and here in front of them was a walking advert for that way of life. And he was smiling like this was the best damned day of his whole brilliant life.

With the hall now full, the soldier started speaking, his American accent as obvious among the British voices as a horn in an orchestra's violin section.

'So, do we have any Infantry here?'

There was a ripple of acknowledgement from the troops, including Liam, but if the soldier had wanted more, he wasn't going to get it. The British, it seemed, were going to play to type and be reserved, which suited Liam perfectly. But not only that, they were knackered. The marine was going to have to work hard to get any response at all. Not that he seemed to care all that much what kind of response he got; he just whooped out with a loud US-style, 'Yeah! Woo-hoo! All right!'

Liam glanced at Cameron. 'Is he for real?'

The marine was speaking again, and he was clearly someone who wasn't just used to people listening to him, but enjoyed making sure they did.

'One thing you all need to understand now that you're out in theatre, and that's the difference between fighting a conventional warfare and engaging in a counter-insurgency.'

Without any warning at all, the marine picked out one of the squaddies in the hall at random and dragged him to the front. Liam could see that the squaddie didn't look best pleased as he stood there like he wanted the world to swallow him whole.

The marine looked at him. 'You're out on patrol, right? Then you receive fire from a compound! Not a village. No civilians. Just a bunch of hard-ass Taliban wanting to bag a few Brits. What are you going to do?'

The British soldier shrugged and said matter-of-factly, 'Return fire.'

At that, the marine swept his arms round to his audience. '*Damn right* we return fire!' he boomed, his voice rolling round the hall like the echo of a cannon. 'We get on that 50-CAL and we blast those fuckers to *hell*!'

Liam sat amazed as the marine then started to make machine-gun sounds. And they were actually pretty accurate; the marine had obviously been practising.

The sergeant turned back to the squaddie he'd dragged to the front. 'But they're still shooting at you, soldier! Rounds are zipping past your head. Someone's been hit! What now?'

The British soldier stalled, and the marine jumped straight in for him.

'We escalate force! Throw some grenades in there! Keep on with that 50-CAL!'

Liam had never witnessed anyone in the military explain anything like this before, and it was certainly a different approach to Major Edwards.

'They're still shooting! Hell, are they ever going to stop? It's seriously kicking off and you're still receiving fire!' boomed the marine. 'So, what are you gonna do then?' He didn't give time for the squaddie next to him to answer but shouted out, 'Call in air support! Let's have at them with a 2,000-pound JDAM – *boom!*'

The JDAM, Liam remembered was a normal unguided gravity bomb, which had bolted onto it a guidance system that allowed it to be guided to a target by GPS. A 2,000lb one would leave one hell of a hole.

As the echo of the marine's voice faded, Liam wasn't sure if he was supposed to cheer or listen or what. Regardless, it was certainly entertaining. Cameron was chuckling beside him, and for a moment Liam thought of Dan – how he would have taken the piss out of this marine. But deep down he knew better; it was no laughing matter.

'Each and every one of you has been given the training to use lethal force, to kill when necessary,' said the marine, calming a little at last, his voice now serious but no less loud. 'But that is conventional warfare. And we've gone beyond that game now. We are in a counter-insurgency and that means different rules.'

Liam knew that this was where it all got complicated. The rules of engagement were being tested time and again and life out here for any soldier was not as simple as getting the enemy in sight and letting rip with a hail of 5.56s and calling in for backup from a swarm of Apache to unleash hell with their 30-millimetre chain gun, Hellfire missiles and Hydra 70 rocket pods.

'Our job,' the marine said, everyone listening in now, 'is to work with and alongside the local population, get them on our side, protect them, and by that I mean being on the side of the government of Afghanistan. That's what'll get us the hell out of here. And the sooner the better, agreed?'

14

With the briefing over, Liam and the rest of the troops were thrown immediately into becoming acclimatized to life in Afghanistan. And that meant getting used to doing everything they'd done back in the cool, damp climate of Britain, working and operating under the same kind of physical and mental pressures, but instead performing it all under the searing heat of the Afghanistan sun.

Liam was marched around the camp in full battle kit. Like any of the soldiers around him, he knew he was fit, but nothing could have prepared him for a heat that was doing its utmost to kill him. The effect of it was exhausting. When he wasn't running kilometre after kilometre, convinced he was going to cough his lungs up, he was still sweating, the stuff pouring out of him and soaking his clothes even when he was just sitting down. All of them were drinking litres and litres of water just to stay hydrated. Back home Liam had become used to the extra thirty kilos he had to carry in theatre, but out in Afghanistan it seemed to have doubled in weight and his legs were continuously drained of all energy. When they were practising an attack or doing a speed march, it only got worse, and Liam couldn't get the water inside himself quick enough. They all carried camel packs – large water reservoirs that formed part of their backpack – and these were quickly drained. At least he wasn't the only one, thought Liam; by the end of the march, they were all half dead.

The one consolation of the frantic timetable was that he didn't get to spend much of it worrying about Mike or what he'd said just before the tour began. They were all too busy and too mentally and physically exhausted to do little more than try and keep up with what was being thrown at them.

Towards the end of their time at Camp Bastion, and in addition to being tipped upside down in a vehicle crash simulator and having to not only get out, but deal with badly injured colleagues, Liam was sat on a bench with Cameron and a number of other soldiers from 2 Rifles, facing yet again the awful reality of the threat of IEDs.

They were in a tent that had the sides partially rolled

up to allow some attempt at ventilation in the constant and searing heat. It wasn't exactly effective, but Liam was more used to the heat by now. In front of them was a sergeant who was also a combat medical technician and it was clear, not just from how he handled himself but also how he spoke, that he had a huge amount of operational experience. Everywhere Liam looked, weapons were at the ready.

The sergeant called the lads to order.

'This, lads, is a run-through of the systematic approach you should take if faced with a casualty.'

Liam had gone through this kind of drill numerous times before, but he still listened in. This was different, he knew that. It was no longer classroom stuff, things he read about in a textbook, but the words of a man who, for all Liam knew, had done exactly what he was about to tell them only hours before.

'So listen in,' continued the sergeant, 'and hopefully you'll learn just enough to save a life. Which is what we all want to do, right?'

Liam, like everyone else, was sipping water. And he was doing it constantly. He was also fully focused on not missing a single word the sergeant said.

'What I'm going to tell you and demonstrate is probably a little different to what you're used to,' said the sergeant, his voice clear and calm, but filled with authority, 'but my aim is to make things better for you out on the ground. I want to give you some simple techniques and procedures that'll help you deal with the worst when it happens. And believe me, for all of you here in front of me, there's a bloody good chance it will.'

Liam knew the statistics as well as anyone sitting around him, with hundreds of British and other Coalition soldiers killed or seriously injured since the move to Helmand in 2006. He was in a dangerous place now. This was no dress rehearsal.

The sergeant was now joined at the front by another soldier. This one, though, was shirtless and wearing shorts, sandals and, for reasons known only to himself, a bright orange wig. He was carrying an M4 carbine.

'Right, this bloke is now out on patrol.'

The soldier grinned.

'Obviously not like this,' said the sergeant, nodding at how the soldier was dressed.

Liam and everyone around him laughed, which despite the serious nature of what they were discussing, and why they were there in the first place, lightened the atmosphere just enough for him to relax.

The sergeant went on as the laughter faded.

'Like I said, he's on patrol, steps on an IED. You've all seen what they are. You all know what these fucking things are capable of. And I bet you could probably even recite to me all the technical shit that you've learned about them, right?'

No one answered. But then it was clear to Liam that the sergeant wasn't expecting them to.

'But what I want you to tell me,' said the sergeant, nodding at the half-naked soldier in the sunglasses, 'is what's going to happen as soon as he stands on that device? What's going to happen to him?'

Everyone was quiet. Liam guessed that, like him, they were all still a little unsure of where they were, even those who had been out before and were on their second or third tour. Camp Bastion was a disorientating place. Also, there was probably a fair amount of not wanting to sound like a total knob by giving the wrong answer.

'The explosion goes as a "V", right?' said the sergeant, answering his own question, and then demonstrating with his hands the shape the blast would take. 'So where's that pressure going to take his arm?'

'Up?' said Liam, his voice joined by those of some of the other soldiers.

'Good,' said the sergeant. 'Absolutely spot-on. And he'll get frag to the side of the chest wall as well. What about the rifle? What's going to happen with that?'

Another soldier called out, 'Hit his head?'

'Dead right,' said the sergeant with a nod. 'It's going to smash into his jawline. And I don't mean just crack it one like a punch in the face from a bloke who doesn't like you in a bar one night. It's going to slam into him with the force of that explosion and break it open. And he's going to get blast ear, maybe even blast lung.'

The list of injuries from the IED was growing, and despite the way the soldier in front of them was dressed, the demonstration was making Liam realize even more just how deadly the devices were. And how quickly they could blow you apart.

The sergeant jabbed a pointed finger towards the soldier's legs. 'He's going to have big chunks missing out of his legs. Blood and bone and all the rest of it everywhere, right? The frag will have slammed into him, mashing everything up. He might even have lost one, maybe both legs. And it's your job to deal with it.'

The sergeant asked the soldier to lie on the floor, then covered his legs in wet mud.

'Like I said, the leg's going to be covered in blood, bits of bone, flesh and in amongst all that the dust just turns to mud. So start washing it down as quickly as you can, got it?'

With a bottle of water, the sergeant quickly cleaned up the leg and pulled out a tourniquet.

'Now put this under the leg and get it nice and tight.'

The sergeant mimed pulling the thing tight on the

soldier's leg. If he'd done it for real, he'd have stopped the blood flowing to the leg, which was the whole point – but it wasn't something you did to a healthy, uninjured leg, of that Liam was sure.

The sergeant looked up from what he was doing. 'I can guarantee, lads, from experience, that you will stop that bleeding if you do it right, and you will make sure he goes home alive.'

Standing up again, the sergeant walked over and grabbed Liam.

'Name?'

'Scott,' answered Liam.

'Right, Scott, come over here, and hold this bloke's hand.'

Liam, surprised by his sudden involvement, did exactly as the sergeant ordered: he knelt down next to the soldier and took his hand.

'Tell me,' said the sergeant, his eyes burrowing into Liam's, 'are you bothered that you're holding another bloke's hand?'

Liam heard the edge in the sergeant's voice. They all did. It wasn't a question, it was a challenge. And a fierce one at that.

Liam shook his head.

The sergeant continued. 'When his legs have been blown to shit?' he continued. 'When he's crying, screaming in agony? Well, lads, any of you got a problem with holding another bloke's hand?'

Liam and everyone else shook their heads.

'Too bloody right you haven't,' the sergeant agreed firmly. 'Because if you have, fuck off now. You're in the wrong job. And I don't want you out there. Why? Simple: a fellow soldier gets injured, then it's your job to keep him calm, talk to him, reassure him, let him know you're there. So don't just grab his arm or shoulder, hold his sodding hand!'

The sergeant paused, took a breath, then spoke once again.

'And if you do your job right, someone will go home who may not have done so if you hadn't been there doing what I've just shown you. Understand?'

A murmur of 'Yes, Sergeant,' was all that was needed.

Everyone understood.

15

Checkpoint 2 was a mud-walled compound stuck out in the Afghanistan countryside. As they'd approached it, Liam had thought how the place looked like some barely standing medieval ruin, the kind that no self-respecting knight would ever use as a shelter, never mind as a fortress. And it was about as welcoming as a disused toilet block. The walls, depending on the sunlight, were either dirty red or dirty brown and were disconcertingly pitted with holes from bullets and mortar rounds.

It had two sangars or sentry posts, each containing a set of seriously powerful binoculars on a tripod, and an L7A2 general-purpose machine gun. The belt-fed GPMG, or 'Gimpy' as it was nicknamed, sending out 7.62 rounds at a rate of 750rpm to a range of 1800 metres, provided fearsome fire support. Liam had spotted various other weapons in the compound, including grenades, mortars and one-shot missile launchers, and one of the Taliban's own weapons of choice: rocket-propelled grenade launchers (RPGs), as well as belt-fed light machine guns and a sniper rifle. The RPG was basic, but in the right hands could easily take out an armoured troop carrier or down a helicopter. Despite the ever-present threat of the Taliban from over the other side of the wall, Liam couldn't stop feeling a little invincible with so much ordnance readily to hand.

Shelter inside the compound comprised a number of large frame tents, their canvas covers seriously worn, and some lean-to structures made from scrappy bits of wood. Plush, it wasn't. And the cookhouse was little more than a few gas burners balanced on bricks along with some huge tins of food.

The compound was surrounded on all sides by fields of maize and poppy, all of which were in the final stages of being harvested. Major Edwards had pointed out to the battalion that because of this the Taliban would, once the harvest was over, go back to what they did best, and in some cases probably enjoyed, which was doing their utmost to kill Coalition troops. He'd left none of them in any doubt that there was a good chance it would be a violent tour. Liam hadn't expected it to be anything else. This was a war zone and he was in it. It was what he'd trained for. All he had to do now was survive it.

All the roads in the local area were little more than badly rutted tracks, often scarred by flooding. In places Liam had seen craters and large sections of road completely destroyed and he guessed this was the result of IEDs. With each one, he wondered who had been injured, how many had died. And if, round the next corner, he would be next.

The fields were all bordered by gullies and ditches, most of which were filled with bushes and tall grass. It was, realized Liam as soon as they arrived, a haven for any Taliban wanting to hide while taking pot shots at a passing squaddie. But as he found and settled into his sleeping area, Liam forced out of his mind all thoughts of his seemingly impossible-to-avoid death by getting his kit sorted out.

Sergeant Reynolds, who was in charge of Liam's group – or multiple – called everyone together. Of the rest of the multiple, Liam knew Cameron and Mike, but as for Lance Corporal Jackson, second-in-command to Sergeant Reynolds, and the five other soldiers, he knew them by name, but little else. He'd been on exercise with all of them, but had really had no chance yet to get to know them beyond the camouflage. This, though, was all about to change, and of that Liam was more than acutely aware.

'Right, to reiterate,' said Sergeant Reynolds, his voice

already dry and raspy with the dust in the air: 'our aim, while we're stuck out here in this fantastic little holiday camp, CP2, is to drive the Taliban into the desert and away from the local population. Is that understood?'

That was probably easier said than done, thought Liam, but he kept his mouth shut.

'And we are to use all methods at our disposal to persuade them to get moving. And I'm assuming I don't really need to explain in detail what I mean by that, right?'

Liam knew exactly what the sergeant was talking about: he meant the gathering of local intelligence and getting to know the local population and protecting them; but also the potential use of force. And if they had to use it to clear the Taliban out, then they would. And from what Liam had seen in the compound, as well as back at Camp Bastion, they had a fairly hefty arsenal to draw from and to call upon as backup.

'I know we've only just arrived,' continued the sergeant, 'but we're not here on a jolly. So you've all got thirty minutes to sort out what's left of your kit. Then we'll be going out on our first foot patrol.'

Liam noticed everyone lean forward. This was it: they weren't just out in a checkpoint; they were about to head off and possibly run into the Taliban.

'First patrol will be me,' said the sergeant, 'Scott,

Dinsdale, White, Allan and Finch, you lucky lads. Allan, radio. And as this is your second tour, Finch, you can be point man.'

Jason Finch, Liam noticed, seemed to smile, like he was happy at the news.

'Lance Corporal Jackson will be staying put,' continued the sergeant. 'With Hacker, Macdonald and Pearce. They'll be up in the sangars until we get back, manning the Gimpys, with their eyes on us, and anything that moves, or looks like it might move, just in case we need to haul arse back here sharpish and they have to put in some covering fire. Any questions?'

Liam had no questions, only relief that for his first patrol, at least, Mike wasn't going with him.

One thing that he had noticed almost immediately when they turned up at Checkpoint 2 was that Sergeant Reynolds had eased off a little. He was still in charge, but he was now treating them as a team of professionals he could depend on and trust, and not simply a group of soldiers he had to whip into shape. It wasn't so much in what he was saying or doing, but the way he was saying or doing it, and already Liam had noticed its effect on the group, making them more at ease with each other and their surroundings, but no less switched on or aware.

The sharp rattle of gunfire snatched Liam from his

thoughts as it peppered the air like firecrackers. Everyone was on their feet in a beat.

'Jackson!' ordered Sergeant Reynolds, his voice calm but firm, pointing up at one of the sangars. 'Get yourself up there now! I want eyes on whoever it is having a go at us and to return fire.' He then turned to the rest of the multiple and nodded at the compound's wall. 'The rest of you, grab your weapons and get up there too! This is it. We're out in the badlands now, not back home on a range playing with blanks. And keep your bloody heads down! I don't want anyone fucking this up and getting their faces shot off on my watch, particularly on our first sodding day, understand?'

Up at the wall, peering through his SUSAT, and with his rifle's safety off, Liam tried to control his breathing and calm himself down. He couldn't see anything in front of them that looked like it was an enemy combatant, not that he was really sure what one would look like. The fields were quiet and the only movement they could see was a couple of tethered goats in the distance slowly munching their way through a dried-out patch of scrub.

More rounds came in, thudding into the walls like fat, drunken bees.

Sergeant Reynolds' voice bellowed across the compound. 'Jackson! You got anything out there? We need to let them know they can't just take pot shots at us!'

'Nothing!' Jackson called back, frustration ringing out clear in his voice. Then, 'No, wait . . . There! Two o'clock. Movement in those bushes!'

Liam and the other soldiers trained their weapons on where the corporal had directed them.

More rounds came in and they all saw the faint spark of muzzle flash from exactly where the corporal had said.

'Return fire!' shouted Sergeant Reynolds. 'Let them know we're here, lads! Have it!'

Liam didn't have to think; he just squeezed the trigger. His rifle kicked, but he was more than used to it now, thanks to all the practice he'd put in, not just during training but also since landing in Afghanistan. He held it firm, training short three-round bursts of fire into the bushes.

'Hold!' shouted Sergeant Reynolds, then shouted for Jackson to have another look.

The compound fell eerily silent. For a moment no further rounds came in.

'Can't see anything,' said Jackson. 'Either he's dead, which I'd prefer, or he's gone to ground, like a shit-scared rabbit.'

'Well, at least we've got something to go check out on our patrol, hey, lads?' said the sergeant, and Liam noticed a hint of excitement in his voice.

With no further evidence of attack, and with everything calm again, what was left of the thirty minutes the sergeant had given them all to sort themselves out zipped by, and Liam was now sitting with the rest of his patrol around a makeshift 3D map of the area surrounding their compound. Lance Corporal Jackson and the others stayed up in the sangars, but as yet no reports had come in of any further movement. Whoever had been shooting was either dead, injured or had slipped away.

Sergeant Reynolds went through the route they were going to take, which involved taking in the position they'd been fired on from earlier, then leading round through a number of fields to another compound, which was apparently a small farm dwelling.

'After we've checked this position to see if there's any evidence of who was firing on us,' he said as he pointed at a basic model of the area he'd put together on the ground, using anything from a mess tin to represent Checkpoint 2, to sticks to mark roads, 'we need to push through here and up to the compound.'

Liam stared at the model, focusing on the route they'd have to take to the compound, which on the sergeant's map was just a large rock. It wasn't just the route he tried to memorize, though, but any major features that he would be able to identify; that would help him make his way back safely if the patrol was split up for whatever reason. It was something he was certain they'd all work hard to avoid, but he'd rather be sure of his route back than find himself out in the fields, alone, with no idea of how to get home to Checkpoint 2, with the Taliban closing in around him, eager for fresh blood.

'If there's no one around, then we need to start being worried,' continued the sergeant, keeping everyone's attention on the model, 'and this alleyway here is looking horrendous, so we all need to be switched on.'

Liam knew what the sergeant was getting at. If there were people around, farmers or whatever just getting on with life, it was a good sign that there were no Taliban in the local area. Because when they moved in to do what they did best and try to kill soldiers, the locals often got wind of it first, and would clear out before anything kicked off. As someone had told them back at Camp Bastion, if the locals suddenly stop using a bridge, there's usually a reason why. And that reason is probably a few kilos of explosive just waiting for you to trigger it.

Talk over, everyone gathered by the battered gate that was the only way into and out of the compound. Jason, a Geordie, who was also the smallest in the multiple and who made up for it by being the loudest mouth of the lot of them, was carrying a combat metal detector and smoking a cigarette. Slung by his side was a black combat shotgun.

'Don't look so worried,' he said as Liam stood by him doing his all not to seem too nervous. 'I can spot an IED at a hundred paces. And this thing can detect not just an IED but someone even just thinking about placing one.' He patted the metal detector like a well-loved pet. 'Where you from, anyway?'

'London,' said Liam.

'Cigarette?'

Liam shook his head as Sergeant Reynolds walked past and over to the gate. Almost as one, each member of the patrol readied their weapons and got into line.

'Finch?' called the sergeant and nodded forwards.

Flicking his cigarette to the ground, Jason walked forward and through the gate. Within a few metres of the compound, heading out on the route they'd discussed, he moved forward, swinging the metal detector left and right.

16

The splatter of blood on the scorched grass, and on the leaves of the bush in front of them, might have already dried in the sun, but the sight was no less awful. Liam knew that none of them had any idea whose bullets had hit home.

'Terry must've scarpered,' said Jason, using the slang term Liam had heard around and about to refer to the Taliban. He was crouching down to examine some scuff marks in the dirt.

To Liam they looked like nothing out of the ordinary, which made him even more glad that he was out here with someone with as much experience as Jason clearly displayed.

'Looks like he went that way,' Jason said, nodding across towards the target compound, 'which is where we're heading anyway, so he might be holed up there when we arrive. Hope so anyway, right? Grabbing ourselves a live one would be a bloody excellent bonus.'

'He's wounded,' said Sergeant Reynolds. 'That'll slow up not just him but whoever he's with, because he'll need medical attention. And you know full well the Taliban don't get taken alive. If he's where we're going and still breathing, you can count on the little bastard having a go at us.'

'Seriously?' said Liam, still staring at the blood. 'He wouldn't want to just stay put and not get found?'

'They don't have a death wish,' said Jason, 'but they don't quit, either. If he's armed and knows he's trapped, he'll kick off, throwing everything he's got at us. And don't go thinking they're crappy fighters, either. They know what they're doing and this place is their home. We're the ones playing catch-up. And sometimes it really fucking shows.'

'Right, let's move out,' said Sergeant Reynolds. 'Everyone, remember your drills and keep your eyes open. We've at least one enemy out there, dead or otherwise, so I'd put money on there being more of them, even if all they're doing is watching to see how we work.'

Liam and the others got ready to move on.

'Finch,' said the sergeant, 'keep that ground sight together, yeah? Yell if you see anything. There's no rush. I'd rather be out here longer and get everyone back in one piece than turn in for an early night, hot chocolate and an episode of *Antiques Roadshow* with one of us minus a leg, got me?'

'Sure thing, boss,' said Jason, and moved off, the detector swinging again with a steady left-right beat.

Liam was three men down from Jason, with John Allan just in front manning the radio, and he had to force himself not to jump every time a branch snapped or a stone shifted underfoot. With each and every step he was sure something was going to explode and end his tour before it had even begun. He'd had nightmares about being blown up. He'd woken up sweating, short of breath, convinced he was dying, blown apart. But he knew this was normal; Cameron had confessed to the same.

Arriving at the other compound without incident, Liam joined in a thorough search of the place. Nothing was found, though: no trace of the wounded Taliban they had expected to find.

'Where do you think he went?' Liam asked as Jason walked over.

'Hopefully nowhere,' said Jason. 'I'd prefer the fucker to be dead than running back to get his mates to come and have a go at us.'

'It'd be good to have a scrap, though,' said Liam, not really meaning his words to be heard. He didn't really want to get into a fight, but a small part of him wanted to be tested.

'Everyone thinks that when they turn up here,' said Jason, and Liam heard the experience in his words. 'You've been trained for it, right? And you want to see if you can handle it.'

Liam nodded, said nothing.

'After a while, though,' continued Jason, 'you begin to realize that the only good thing that can come out of any of this is that you get through each day and each night, then go home in one piece to a pint of beer, a warm bed and, if you're lucky, a shag.'

Saying no more, he led them all back to the compound. After a quick debrief by Sergeant Reynolds they all went to their sleep areas.

'It's a little bit different to doing a foot patrol at Catterick, isn't it?' said Cameron. 'I'd almost think about using the word "exciting" if it hadn't been so bloody terrifying.'

Liam was relieved to hear someone else admit to having been nervous as well.

'You reckon that Taliban is still out there?' he asked, imagining whoever it was getting ready for another attack, probably with reinforcements.

'Dead, I reckon,' said Cameron. 'We tore that position apart. I was amazed we didn't find a body. Not that

I wanted to, but I just don't see how anyone got out of that alive.'

Liam had wondered the same but had kept the thought to himself.

'By the way,' said Cameron, 'Reynolds has decided in his wisdom to put me in the cookhouse for a few days. So I'll be doing the chef thing for us. Any requests?'

'Yeah,' said Liam. 'That you don't do any of the cooking. You're shit at it.'

'I'm hurt.'

Liam smiled. 'What's for dinner then? Roast beef and Yorkshire pudding? That's all you live on back home, right, Dinsdale?'

Cameron looked thoughtful. 'Nice idea,' he said, 'but to be honest, I think I'll probably just go for some nice brown tasteless slop. With lumps in. And rice.'

'I can't wait.'

Cameron walked over to his own bed and sat down and Liam got on with sorting his kit. The weight of everything still felt cumbersome, and he knew running with it would slow him down hugely, but it didn't feel half as bad as it had when they'd arrived at Camp Bastion. With his pack off, Liam double-checked that his rifle was safe, then went to lay out his sleeping bag, which was all scrunched up.

Flicking it back, something flew out at Liam and he

jumped back instinctively. All he could make out was big, hairy insect legs, and whatever it was, he managed to slap it away before it landed in his face.

Cameron looked over. 'What the hell's wrong with you? What happened?'

Liam stared down at what had been, only moments earlier, tucked up in his bed.

'That was in my stuff,' he said, pointing at the dead thing in the dirt. 'A big fucking spider!'

'It's a camel spider,' said Cameron, kicking it with his boot. 'You must've killed it.'

Liam had never seen anything like it in the flesh, not even in a zoo – it was like something out of a horror movie; there were pictures of the things all over the internet, posted by soldiers on tour. The creature was enormous, larger than his own hands. They weren't deadly, but the bites were nasty and had a habit of getting infected real quick out in the desert heat.

'I only slapped it away,' he said. 'It must've been dead already.'

'You sure?'

'Reckon so,' said Liam, calm at last.

'So how did it get into your bag, then?'

Liam frowned. 'What you saying?'

'I'm not,' said Cameron. 'These things are everywhere. I'm surprised you didn't see one back at Camp

Bastion. It probably just got caught up in your kit and died in transit.' He nudged it again with his foot. 'Ugly, isn't it?'

Liam wasn't so sure, though, and without waiting for Cameron he walked out into the middle of the compound.

Cameron joined him. 'What's up with you?'

Liam nodded over at Mike, who was still up in one of the sangars.

'Bollocks,' said Cameron. 'You're paranoid.'

'Am I?' asked Liam.

Cameron shrugged and said, 'Well, if that's the best he can do . . .'

Liam knew Cameron had a point. Out here they all had more important things on their mind. And Mike, since they'd arrived in Afghanistan, had been nothing other than the professional soldier.

As Cameron headed over to the cookhouse, Liam wandered back to his bed, tossed the camel spider over the wall and sat down. He had no proof Mike had put the spider in his kit, but that wasn't going to stop him being wary. And he had a sense that this was only the beginning.

Liam quickly realized that the first day was simply a taster before the main course. Three weeks in and not a day had gone by without contact with the enemy. Mostly it was sniper rounds, or someone taking a pot shot at the compound by spraying a magazine's worth in their general direction, their bullets doing little more than slapping uselessly into the walls, but it was more than enough to keep everyone on their toes. Neither was it simply a daytime activity, the Taliban using the cover of darkness and the fact that the multiple weren't going to be moving outside the walls of the compound as a good excuse to come at them time and time again. With each night passing, and when he wasn't manning one of the sangars, trying to spot movement in the dark that would signal that an attack was imminent, Liam soon got used to grabbing a kip whenever he could. It had become very apparent that a full night's sleep was something none of them would get again, at least not until the tour was over and they were back at what now seemed like the luxury of Camp Bastion.

Liam soon lost count of the number of times he'd heard the telltale whistle of a bullet slipping through the air close to his head. A few RPGs had been sent their way as well, but one had failed to explode, and the other two had missed by a country mile, exploding way wide of their target, much to the amusement of Liam and the others. Death, it seemed, was at times something that was almost fun to dodge, to be laughed at, rather than possibly round the next corner.

Out on patrol, Jason stuck with being point man. Liam knew that they were supposed to rotate and give him a rest, but he, like everyone else, agreed that he was the best at it, his ground sight better than any of them, and they all felt much safer when he was out front. And Jason wasn't complaining either.

Having been told of the terror of IEDs, and trained in how to deal with them, Liam was pleased that so far Jason had found only two. And with each device found the counter-IED team had been flown out from Camp Bastion to deal with them. This extended the foot patrols by hours, but he didn't care. All that mattered was that they got back to their compound with everyone intact.

For Liam, though, the one thing bothering him above all was that Mike was still messing with him. At least, he assumed it was Mike. He'd find bits of his kit had gone missing and would turn up randomly in another part of the compound. Or stuff would simply move, such as his wash kit. It was never dangerous stuff, like his magazines or grab bag filled with his first-aid kit – he guessed that Mike was too professional a soldier to do anything that could compromise operational duties – but it was enough to get on his nerves. He still had no proof that it was Mike, and until he did, all he could do was keep his mouth shut and just focus on the job in hand.

With their time eventually over at Checkpoint 2, Liam and the rest of the multiple rotated to Checkpoint 3.

'It's worse than CP2,' said Liam as he walked into the compound, the rest of the multiple filing in behind him. 'How can that be in any way fucking possible?'

His heart sank into his already worn boots, the soles of which were starting to come away thanks to the battering they were getting. The walls of Checkpoint 3 were in even more of a dilapidated state than those back at Checkpoint 2, and he wondered just how much protection they would afford in an enemy crossfire.

'Massive understatement,' said Cameron and turned to Sergeant Reynolds. 'Sure this is the right place, boss? Looks like it's been abandoned for weeks. And I'm sure I phoned ahead asking for the five-star treatment. You know – spa, room service, white dressing gown, bath oils . . . a bit of luxury, right?'

'It's the right place, I'm afraid,' said Reynolds who, Liam noticed, had continued to grow more human since being out in Afghanistan. Back in the UK he'd thought him a complete tosser, just a grumpy sod who liked picking soldiers up on what they were doing wrong just for the hell of it. Out here, though, on the front line, he was a good soldier and a strong leader. And Liam had learned a lot just from watching him. He trusted him too, which was a good thing.

'Least they could've done is leave us some flowers,' said Jason, heading over to where they would be sleeping. 'Not even a chocolate on the bed. Rubbish.'

'And it stinks too,' said White.

'Sure that's not you, Gandalf?' said John Allan, a soldier from the Territorials who was covered in tattoos and whose job back home was working for a tyre-fitting company. Out here he was responsible for the radio.

Paul White was the oldest in the group, but the nickname had come from the fact that he was almost totally grey, and in the morning his stubble was thick enough to be a beard. He was also a medic.

Paul punched John on the arm, then strode over to a bed and sat down. 'It's like Room 101,' he said.

Liam asked, 'How do you mean?'

'It's a room that contains everyone's worst nightmare,' said Paul. 'And if you ask me, that's this place. What a shit hole.'

A few days into life at Checkpoint 3, and Liam and the rest had all settled into the same routine of foot patrols, meetings with locals to gather intelligence, manning the checkpoint, personal admin, and all the other mundane stuff that came with living out in the field. Though increasingly aware of just how good his training had been – the days spent at the Afghan village in Norfolk, as well as the days out on the range – Liam had soon found that the excitement of all that Boy Scout stuff, eating off stoves and living under the stars, quickly faded. He wanted a comfy bed, good food and a beer. Jason, he realized, had been right.

What made it worse was that since arriving at Checkpoint 3 there hadn't been a single contact with any Taliban, which seemed odd: life at Checkpoint 2 had been a case of constant, if not overly accurate or violent, contact. Liam could tell that everyone was getting edgy, including himself. It wasn't that he wanted to be shot at. It was just that it seemed strange that no one was even coming to try and have a go.

'Like the rest of you,' said Sergeant Reynolds, with the others from the multiple gathered around him, 'I don't like it here. The place is a dump and the sooner we're out of it, the better. But until then, we have to stick to task.'

A murmur of agreement shuffled through Liam and the others.

'Above all, though, what's bothering me is how quiet it is. I don't like it. None of us do.'

'Something's brewing, boss,' said Jason. 'I can smell it.'

'That's Dinsdale's cooking,' said Paul. 'Burns everything.'

Sergeant Reynolds raised a hand to still the laughter. 'I'm with you on this, Finch,' he said. 'Something's definitely brewing. So we need to be even more switched on than usual, OK? I don't want the Taliban thinking we've slackened off because they've gone quiet.'

Evening was drawing in and a bright moon was now visible in the sky.

'We've got nothing from the locals,' said Cameron. 'Whatever the Taliban are up to, they're keeping it quiet.'

'Well, we'll just have to stay alert, won't we, Dinsdale?' said Sergeant Reynolds. 'If and when it kicks off, I don't want any of us making stupid errors, got me?'

Everyone nodded agreement.

The following morning, after another night of absolutely nothing happening, Liam was up in one of the sangars manning a GPMG with Cameron, who was staring through the binoculars. As usual, nothing was happening and they were bored.

'It's dead out there,' said Cameron, scanning the

ground around the compound. 'Where the hell are they?'

Liam turned to reply when the familiar sound of a round coming in snapped the moment in two and a bullet thunked into a plank of wood behind him.

17

'Muzzle flash!' yelled Cameron. 'Ten o'clock!'

Liam had seen it too and he swung the GPMG round to return fire on the position. The weapon jumped a little, but it was easy to keep under control. With each squeeze of the trigger, he sent out a hail of rounds to where both he and Cameron had seen the flash of a weapon being fired. The ground exploded in a cloud of dust as the rounds slammed into the dirt, ripping it apart in moments.

Liam eased off.

'Dinsdale, you see anything?'

'Nothing,' said Cameron, when another round came in, this time sending up a hail of dirt from the compound wall right in front of the binoculars.

'The sod's moved!' shouted Liam, pointing out into the countryside in front of them. 'That came from out to the right!'

Cameron swung the binoculars round.

'You see him?' asked Liam.

Cameron was silent, then called out, 'Sighted! He's behind that hut at one o'clock!'

The rest of the lads were now up and looking over the wall of the compound, with Sergeant Reynolds at the other lookout.

'Got him!' shouted the sergeant. 'Contact confirmed! Come on, lads! We're on! Have it!'

Everyone opened fire, pasting the spot with bullets. The hut, which as Liam had seen from numerous patrols was a simple structure of thin, crumbling mud walls with a wooden roof balanced precariously on top, shuddered violently as it was peppered with rounds. A bit of the roof fell in like it had simply had enough and given up.

'Stop!' shouted Sergeant Reynolds.

Checkpoint 3 fell silent.

'Dinsdale, any movement?'

'He's either down or gone,' Cameron called back. He then looked up at Liam. 'That was too close,' he said. 'That bastard nearly slotted us both!'

Sergeant Reynolds called the multiple together. 'Right, we need to get a foot patrol out there now, either to confirm a kill, or bring the injured shooter back and get him medevac'd to Camp Bastion. At which point his life will become a hell of a lot more fucking complicated.' Reynolds nodded at Corporal Jackson. 'You, get up there with Dinsdale,' he ordered, pointing up to one of the sangars, then looked to Macdonald and Pearce. 'And you two, in the other. I want eyes on that hut and I don't want you to even blink in case you fucking well miss them! Any movement, I want to know. And be ready for me calling in for fire support.'

As Corporal Jackson and Cameron went back up to the sangar, Liam and the rest went into autopilot and were soon kitted up and ready at the gate to move out. Every patrol since arriving at Checkpoint 3 had been a wasted journey and Liam had started to get bored. Not complacent; just tired of walking out and finding nothing. He wasn't looking for a fight, or to get shot at, but he could tell that they had all started to feel the tension building. Now though, knowing they were going out to actively track down an enemy combatant? He was nervous, but he was also excited. This is what they had all trained for.

Jason was once again point man and led the way out slowly, carefully, through the gate. Liam, who was behind Mike, pushed his nerves down and kept his eyes on the hut, fully expecting incoming rounds at any moment.

After a slow, uneventful walk, they arrived at the hut.

A call came from Jason: 'Nothing here. Terry's scarpered!'

Then the familiar sound of a round coming in cracked the air.

Jason hit the deck, then yelled back to Sergeant Reynolds, 'Where the hell did that come from?'

Liam and the others scanned the surrounding area, Liam using his SUSAT to get a better look and hopefully spot something.

Another round came in, this one whistling over Liam's head like a jet-propelled wasp.

'Over there!' shouted Paul, pointing to a small compound about a hundred metres further on behind the hut.

As far as Liam knew, the place had until a few weeks ago been occupied by an old farmer. They'd searched it and found nothing of importance, no hint of activity by the Taliban. It was, as far as they could tell, just abandoned. Now, though, things had clearly changed. And Liam knew there was no way they were just going to let the shooter get away to come back again and have another go at them. That wasn't the way this worked.

Sergeant Reynolds called over: 'Dinsdale! Suppressing fire! Keep that fucker's head down! And if it does show, then just knock it off his fucking shoulders!'

The thick, rapid rattle of the GPMG brought to life by Cameron soon echoed around Liam and the others. With the sniper now pinned down, they moved on. Liam's senses seemed more alert as they made their slow way forwards. He was aware of smells in the air that he usually didn't notice or just took for granted or had grown used to: the hay-like smell of the dry shrubs and grass they were moving through, gun oil from his weapon, the acrid smell of spent rounds in the air, his own sweat. It was as if all the little bits of the world around him had become more obvious, shouting out to him to be noticed. Even the tread of the boots of John, who was now in front of him, seemed clearer, more precise, and as they drew up to the compound he could hear his heart, but it was a controlled beat, strong and sure, not rapid and panicked.

A few moments later, Liam was crouched with the others in a ditch, all of them spaced out about ten to fifteen paces apart. It was dusty, more so than out in the open, and the ditch was filled with roots and twigs that seemed to just spring out and hook into him no matter how or where he crouched.

Readying himself for the advance on the compound, Liam made to get up on his feet when heavy machine-gun fire exploded from all directions. The ground around the patrol was stitched by bullets, the air filled with the whine of rounds speeding by and all too close.

The ground shuddered under Liam, a sign that the bullets were landing within a metre of where he was now squatting. And that wasn't good. These weren't shots sent out in a random spray in the hope that they might hit something. Whoever was firing knew exactly where they were and was closing in for a kill.

'Where the hell is that coming from?' shouted Sergeant Reynolds.

Liam quickly scanned the area, then ducked back down. Muzzle flash was coming from everywhere but the compound ahead. And he knew that they all had a fair idea what that meant: they'd been drawn out into an ambush. And now here they were, in the kill zone.

'We need to get to cover fast,' ordered the sergeant, pointing at the compound. 'We go in twos, fire and manoeuvre, you know the drill. Hacker, Scott? Shift it!'

It was simple, but it worked and could be used in advance or retreat. One of them would provide suppressing fire, to keep the enemy's heads down, and the other would move. Then they'd switch until their objective was achieved, be that either killing the enemy, or escape. They'd all practised it enough but now, Liam realized, it was probably going to save his life.

'Scott! Go!'

It was Mike shouting, and Liam, aware now that for

the first time since arriving in Afghanistan he was fighting alongside a man he thought was looking for a chance to kill him, was up on his feet and running, rifle at the ready and firing quick three-round bursts. He knew it was against everything in the book to fire while moving but at that moment he didn't care. If it stopped him getting shot, it was worth the bollocking from Reynolds later.

Grabbing cover behind a smashed tree, Liam dropped to his knee and opened fire. A couple of seconds later, Mike raced past and a few paces later did the same. Liam was up, running, firing; dropped down, kept firing. He changed magazines but didn't miss a beat. Then they were inside the compound, out of breath, adrenaline racing, and wired to getting back to the checkpoint.

'It's a fucking trap,' said Mike, hissing the words through his teeth, voicing exactly what Liam had been thinking. 'They lured us here. A bloody ambush!'

Liam flicked his eyes around the compound. The place was little more than a crude set of walls made up of two main areas divided by another wall, through which a rough door gave access from one to the other. There was no roof. However, a mud-walled shelter lay in the area they were currently standing in, little larger than a garden shed. A fire was still smouldering in a pit dug into the rough ground.

Paul and Jason arrived, their eyes wide and alert, like wolves on the hunt.

'They're all around us,' said Jason, breathing hard. 'I think Gandalf slotted one, but we didn't bother checking. Only way we're getting out of this is if we fight our way out.'

The sound of gunfire continued as Sergeant Reynolds and John, who was carrying the radio, sprinted in.

'Right, all of you, get up on that wall and return fire!' ordered the sergeant. 'And get eyes on where the Taliban are. Find out where those fuckers are holed up! If I have to, I'll call in air support.'

Liam legged it and heaved himself up onto a pile of junk in the corner of the compound; Mike was doing the same further down. Rifle at the ready, he raised himself above the wall and opened fire. But instead of seeing muzzle flash, Liam saw someone leap out from behind a far-off tree with something slung over his shoulder pointing directly at him. It was an RPG, a silhouette any of them would recognize anywhere.

The world stopped. All Liam was aware of was that deadly weapon now pointing right at him. Nothing else mattered.

He dropped from where he was standing like his legs had snapped.

'RPG! RPG! Incoming! INCOMING!'

Everyone hit the deck. Dust kicked up into Liam's mouth, his eyes, as he tried desperately to get as low as possible, to make like the ground.

The RPG slammed into the wall and the dull thump of the explosion lifted him off the ground and sucked the air from his lungs. Mud rained down all around and he could see nothing but dust, his ears ringing from the blast, as he choked to get a breath. Then another round came in, crashing into the same section of the wall, and Liam choked on even more dust as rubble and dirt blasted outwards.

Blinking away the sand and grit in the air, Liam scrambled to his feet. Not only could he hardly see, but the area around him was also unrecognizable. Rock and rubble were strewn everywhere, dust filled the air and he couldn't see more than a metre or so in front of him. He stumbled as he tried to move, tripped over a rock and slammed into the ground, a sharp pebble stabbing hard into his knee. He had no idea which way to run to get out of trouble.

Rounds thwacked into the ground close by and Liam quickly got himself out of the way. He couldn't stay where he was, of that he was sure, but he had no idea where to go to get himself out of the way and stop himself getting shot to pieces. He was pinned down.

He tried shouting for Mike, his backup, but his voice

caught in his throat, bone-dry and choked with the dust. Panic twisted his gut. What if he was cut off from the others? What if they'd gone off and, in the confusion, left him behind? What if they couldn't see him and he got caught in the crossfire? What if he was captured by the Taliban, tortured . . . he'd heard the rumours that the Taliban were actively looking to get themselves a British soldier. And everyone knew where that would lead – a starring role in a movie of your own death, probably involving a sharp knife sawing away at your neck.

Liam pushed the horror of that image away and forced himself to calm down. The only thing panic was going to do was get him killed. No way would the rest of the patrol leave him behind, he knew that for sure. He had to get a grip, remember his drills, and get out fast.

Liam caught sight of a silhouette coming towards him. When the dust cleared a little he realized who it was.

'Mike . . .'

For a second, he was relieved – not that it was Mike, but that it was one of the patrol. At least he wasn't alone. Then he saw what Mike was holding. Not his own SA80, but an AK47, the Taliban's other weapon of choice, not just because it was accurate, but because it was famously reliable and robust. You could run over one in a tank and it would still empty a magazine without much bother.

'Where the hell did you find that?'

'Taliban must've been using this place after all,' said Mike. 'Those RPGs uncovered a stash of weapons.'

More gunfire echoed all around, but Mike, Liam noticed, was unconcerned. Then he levelled the weapon.

'What are you doing, Mike?'

Mike didn't respond, just came a little closer, the barrel of the AK47 pointing straight at Liam's chest.

'Mike . . .'

Mike readied the weapon in his hands, no emotion in his face, his eyes dead and staring.

'Soldiers die, Liam,' he said, and it didn't pass Liam by that Mike had used his first name. It sounded even more ominous out here where they were. 'Out here, it's like you said, remember? Risk is part of the job?'

Liam started to back away, but he was already at a disadvantage. Mike had his weapon trained on him and Liam knew he wouldn't have a chance even to get a shot off.

'Stop pissing around, Mike!' he shouted. 'You've made your point, OK? I'm sorry about Dan. We shouldn't have been up there. What more do you want?'

THE NEW RECRUIT

Mike raised the weapon. 'Take a guess . . .'

Then, just as Liam was sure Mike was about to empty the weapon into his chest, the familiar and deadly sound of an RPG cut into the moment and the world between Liam and Mike shattered completely.

18

At first, all Liam was aware of was that he was moving and that he wasn't doing it himself. His ears were ringing, he could hardly see, the world around him blurry and clouded like it was shrouded in thick fog. He could taste blood and dust and grit in his mouth, and something was pulling him across rough ground. He looked left, right, tried to force his eyes to focus as he rapidly blinked away the muck that was choking his vision. A field? What the hell was he doing being dragged across a field? Where was he?

Voices. No, it was one voice. And it was talking to him. The others were more distant and they were shouting. And there was another sound too. A sort of percussive sound, like peas being dropped onto a snare drum.

'Liam? Liam! Thank God you're all right! We're getting you out of here. Don't worry, mate! Just stay with us . . .'

Something had happened to him, but what? He remembered explosions, Mike – but there was something else too; he just couldn't trace it in his mind. Then his eyes opened, pulled everything into focus, saw it was Paul who was talking to him, and he remembered exactly where he was.

'Gandalf! What the fuck happened? Where's Mike? He—'

Liam's voice got snagged in his throat, choked to silence. He couldn't speak. The dragging sensation stopped. He sat up, coughing a thick black slew of grime and grit and blood out of his mouth. What had happened was still foggy, unclear. But Mike was a part of it. Something weird had happened, something wrong. Very wrong indeed.

'It was Mike,' he said again, trying to sort through his muddled memories, trying to comprehend what had just happened.

'Take it easy,' said Paul. 'We're nearly back at the compound. Reynolds has called in air support.'

'No, I mean, it was Mike!' replied Liam, his voice sharp and scared this time, his gut telling him that it wasn't right, but he didn't get to finish as they all saw a huge section of countryside burst upwards like a volcano erupting. The shockwave tore through the air, slamming into Liam and sucking the breath from his lungs. He gasped, found air again.

'That should give them a headache,' said Paul, standing up and heaving Liam to his feet. 'Lean on me, Scott. It's not far. And I know I'm old, but I'm still fitter than most of you young fuckers.'

Then they were moving, Paul setting the pace, Liam trying to get some life back into his legs.

The compound came into view. Liam saw Cameron in the sangar manning the GPMG and sending out repeated bursts of fire back from where they'd come. He looked every inch the soldier he'd been trained to be. Focused and professional, fierce.

Ahead, the gate swung open and Sergeant Reynolds yelled out, 'Move it, Gandalf! Get Scott inside now!'

With the sound of the gate slamming shut behind them, Liam was for a moment overwhelmed with relief. Whatever had just happened, he'd somehow survived it. And being alive had never felt so good.

Paul laid Liam down on the nearest bed.

'I still don't know what happened,' said Liam, his head woozy and spinning like he'd been out on the piss. 'Mike—'

'Don't move,' ordered Paul. 'You were knocked out by an RPG explosion. And you were bloody lucky it didn't take your head off, so I don't want you messing up by falling over and cracking your skull open, under-stand?'

Liam nodded weakly. He was feeling dazed now and glad to be off his feet. His stomach was close to turning itself inside out and he was focusing hard on not chucking up all over his boots.

Paul returned with a grab bag stuffed full of medical kit. He dropped down in front of Liam and shone a small Maglite in his eyes.

'Name, rank, number,' he said, switching off the torch.

Liam responded accordingly.

'Where are you?'

'Listen, Gandalf—' began Liam, but Paul cut him off.

'Answer the fucking question, Scott.'

'Afghanistan,' said Liam. 'Room 101, I mean CP3.'

Paul nodded. 'Good,' he said. 'How do you feel? Dizzy? Headache?'

Liam nodded. 'Like I've been head-butted by a rhino.'

'You've got concussion,' said Paul. 'You'll be out of action for a couple of days, just so we can keep an eye on you.'

Liam made to protest, but Paul held up a hand to shut him down.

'We can't afford to have you dropping on us during a patrol,' he said, 'or getting dizzy in a firefight. You'd be as much a danger to us like that as any incoming fire. It's precautionary. So why don't you be a good little soldier, shut the hell up and take these.' He handed Liam two large tablets and a bottle of water. Liam necked them, squeezed his eyes shut, then flicked them open again. His memory was still refusing to clear, but his gut was still twisting itself up about something.

'So, Gandalf, what actually happened?'

'It was a trap,' said Paul. 'We were pinned down. They were throwing everything they could at us. You escaped two RPGs but the third knocked you flat. We found you covered in rubble. The compound's still standing, though it's got a few big holes in it now. You're one lucky bastard, you know that?'

'I was with Mike – I mean Hacker,' said Liam.

'He's fine,' said Paul. 'You were the one who was knocked unconscious.'

Liam screwed his eyes shut again to force his brain to give up the information he so desperately wanted: an accurate memory of what had really happened rather than just what Paul and the others had found.

'You sure you're all right?' asked Paul.

Then, at last, his mind cleared and Liam remembered, and the memory of it came crashing down on him like a smashed window.

'There was a weapons stash,' he said. 'It was hidden in the wall.'

'We found it,' said Paul.

'No, that's not what I meant!' said Liam, his voice rising now, images downloading into his mind at light speed. 'Hacker found them. He had an AK47.'

'We found half a dozen AKs,' said Paul. 'And some other stuff. Been right under our noses ever since we got here. Sneaky little sods.'

Liam spotted Mike. He was sitting on his own bed, turned away from them. Before Paul could react, Liam was up and charging across the compound. He grabbed Mike and threw him across the ground.

'What the hell were you going to do with that AK47, Mike? What? You wanted to kill me? Is that it?'

Mike held up his hands to fend Liam off. 'What the hell are you talking about? Have you gone nuts? The RPG knock your brain out of your skull?'

Liam wasn't listening. 'You switched weapons so no one would know,' he said, going in again for Mike, who was now pushing himself backwards across the ground with his heels. 'You could just say I was hit by some stray Taliban rounds. An unfortunate accident.

I'm right, aren't I? Just bloody well admit it!'

'I swear I don't know what you're talking about,' Mike replied, as Paul jumped in between them. 'White, get this little nutter off me!'

'Stand down, Scott!' shouted Paul. 'Just back off!'

Liam was having none of it. 'He was going to shoot me, Gandalf!' he shouted and tried to push past, but Paul stood fast and immovable.

Sergeant Reynolds raced over. 'What the hell's going on?'

'That fucker tried to kill me!' snarled Liam, jabbing a finger at Mike, who was now off the ground and standing just far enough away to be out of reach. 'He found the AK47s. He levelled one at me, then the RPG round came in and—'

The sergeant silenced Liam with a raised hand and a hard look. It was a look no one ever argued with.

'That's a serious allegation so you'd better think carefully about what you're saying, Scott.'

'And it's total bollocks,' said Mike with a sneer of utter disgust. 'He's remembering it wrong.'

The sergeant looked at Mike. 'Well, Hacker?'

'I found the weapons, that much is right,' said Mike. 'Liam must've seen me grabbing them, that's all I can think of. He's confused. Maybe his injury's worse than White thinks.'

'Liar!' shouted Liam, and again made to close the gap with Mike.

Sergeant Reynolds got in Liam's way and faced him down. 'Calm down, soldier! And I mean it! Get a grip!'

Liam snapped his mouth shut, but kept his eyes on Mike. If he could've turned the stare into bullets, he would've done.

For a moment, no one said a word.

'Here's what we're going to do,' said the sergeant, now that he had everyone's attention. 'Hacker, Scott, you're going to stay away from each other until you, Scott, calm the fuck down. Understand?'

Liam said nothing, didn't move his eyes from Mike.

'I want to talk to both of you so I can work out exactly what happened. Any questions?'

Liam shook his head.

'Good. Now get back to your own bed, Scott. Immediately. I'll be over soon enough.'

Following the sergeant's orders, Liam left Mike and lay down, shielding his eyes from the sun with his arms. He replayed over and over what had happened, tried to see if he had been mistaken, but no matter which way he looked at it, all he could see was Mike, the AK47 in his hands and the barrel pointing directly at his chest. Even if his intent had been only to scare him, Liam was still unnerved. If Mike was willing to go this far, then what would he try next?

A voice interrupted his thoughts. It was Sergeant Reynolds.

'Any clearer?'

Liam shrugged. 'I'm only saying what happened,' he said. 'I'm not lying.'

'I trust you realize that what you're suggesting, if it proved to be true, would have Hacker in prison?'

'But I can't prove it, can I?' said Liam. 'It's his word against mine.'

'Exactly,' said the sergeant. 'Which means all I've got in front of me is you kicking off and threatening to beat the crap out of Hacker. It's not much, Scott, and it looks seriously bloody crazy from where I'm standing. Care to explain any further? Is there a problem here between you and Hacker?'

Liam stared into the middle distance. He was cornered. What Mike had done, he couldn't prove. There was nothing he could do about it. And there was no point explaining the shit between them. The sergeant wouldn't be interested. And who could blame him? It was history. All that mattered was looking after each other's back and getting the hell out of Afghanistan alive and in one piece, or as close to as possible.

'If we were back in barracks, I'd take this further,' said

Sergeant Reynolds. 'And by further, I mean have you marched out of the barracks for the rest of your career, understand?'

Liam nodded. And he believed the sergeant utterly.

'But out here, I've not got that luxury, have I? I'm supposed to have twelve men, but instead I've got nine under my command. Good ones, Scott, and that goes for you too. I cannot afford to lose any of you. Or have you fighting amongst yourselves. It's bad enough having the Taliban trying to kill us without you trying it as well.'

Liam shuffled on his bed. All he really wanted at that moment was to be left alone.

'So for now I'm giving you a verbal warning. Which is worth about as much as the paper it's not written on. But if you pull a stunt like that again, Scott, you'd better believe I'll have you not just kicked out of this multiple, but out of Afghanistan. And I'll do it so bloody hard you won't need an aircraft to get you home. Are we clear on that?'

Liam nodded. 'Yes, boss.'

Sergeant Reynolds stood up, but his eyes didn't leave Liam.

'Whatever it is between you two that brought this on, I don't want to hear of it ever again. So pull your head out of your arse, and get soldiering. That's all that you should be thinking of right now. You've had the training and you're bloody good at it, so stay focused, Scott. And believe me, doing that is more than enough. Agreed?'

Then he turned away and walked out into the compound, leaving Liam alone with his thoughts and a worrying sense that Mike wasn't just out to mess with his mind: he wanted him dead.

19

'We've got no choice,' said Sergeant Reynolds to Liam and the others. 'For whatever reason, we won't be able to rotate and get back to Patrol Base 4 for another couple of weeks at least.'

'If you don't mind me saying so, boss,' said Jason, who was scratching dry sweat off his forehead, 'that's complete and total bollocks.'

It was late afternoon, the multiple had just received some bad news, and Liam's morale, just like everyone else's, had taken a real kick in the balls. It was one thing trying to keep his mind on the job after what had happened with Mike, but now something else had come along to make everything a whole lot worse.

Like everyone else, Liam had been looking forward to getting out of Room 101 and heading to Patrol Base 4. There, they would be able to enjoy some decent food, air conditioning, fresh water. Even a shower. Now, though, it looked like that wasn't going to happen.

'But we've already sat out here on our arses longer than we should've done,' said Paul, joining in. 'Supplies are low. And I don't mean just the food. Our medical supplies are fuck all use if we get hit hard. We were low on ammo when we arrived and it's only getting worse. If we get into a serious firefight, the last thing we should be thinking about is if we've got enough ammo or not.'

'And Allan for one could do with a proper shower,' said Cameron. 'Stinks like he sleeps in a barrel of shit.'

John didn't laugh. No one did, because there really wasn't anything to laugh about. Even Liam, who generally found most of what Cameron said funny, was silent. The ammo situation was on everyone's mind the most. Crap food they could put up with – even the stench from the wag bags for shitting in – but if their ability to defend themselves was compromised, the consequences were unimaginable. Trouble was, Liam knew that they were all busy imagining it.

'We've just got to deal with it,' said Sergeant Reynolds, his voice firm. 'And the only difference complaining is going to make is to get in the way of what we're out here to do. So I want all of you to keep your game up, understand? Keep it together.'

A muttered 'Yes, boss,' was given by Liam and the rest.

'If anything, step it up,' continued the sergeant. 'I don't want any stupid mistakes made just because we're all pig sick of the hotel. And when you do fire your weapons, make those rounds count. Don't go just spraying metal all over the countryside like you're John fucking Rambo blowing the shit out of Russians.' He took a deep breath before going on, 'Now that's dealt with, I want some decent supper, and while that's being cooked, the rest of us need to be busy. And by busy I mean making sure your kit's sorted, stripping your weapons, readying yourself for whatever – got it? Jackson, you and Scott go in one sangar; Hacker, I want you and Gandalf in the other.'

Meeting over, the eight soldiers got to task. As Liam made his way after Corporal Jackson, he sent a nod to Cameron, who was back in the cookhouse, not because he was good at cooking, but because he was the least shit at it.

'Yorkshire puds again tonight, is it? Getting a bit samey, if you ask me.'

'Beggars can't be choosers,' replied Cameron. 'And I've been down to the cellar to find a few decent bottles of red. Eight for eight-thirty OK? I'll reserve you a table.'

'Perfect,' said Liam, leaving Cameron to rustle up yet another big bowl of pasta-based slop as he headed up to the lookout.

Corporal Jackson was already on the binos.

'Anything?' asked Liam.

Jackson shook his head. 'Been quiet this past few days. Nothing happening anywhere.'

'It's like we've been forgotten,' said Liam. 'Maybe the Taliban don't see the point of hitting us again. Bigger stuff elsewhere or something.'

Jackson didn't move from the binos. 'Either that,' he said, 'or they're planning something.'

Liam went over to the GPMG, readied the weapon, got himself comfortable and stared out across the fields.

The land around the checkpoint was bathed in an eerie half-light, like the place had become permanently trapped somewhere between day and night, a grey world just this side of hell. It was an odd and gloomy evening, thought Liam, and shadows seemed to droop from the trees like lengths of old rag. There was no movement anywhere, almost as though the local population had taken all the wildlife and just moved out completely. It was silent, like the whole place was waiting expectantly for a funeral procession to drive past. Liam wondered for a moment why, if it was so quiet, supplies couldn't be flown in, but he knew that it was all down to priorities. They were a little CP out in the badlands with nothing much going on. Time and money and bullets were better spent elsewhere. It didn't mean that they were forgotten, just further down the list.

'You and Hacker settled down?' asked Jackson. 'That was some serious shit you accused him of a couple of days ago. What the hell were you thinking?'

Liam was doing his best to either avoid Mike or not think about him, but it wasn't easy – it wasn't like he could just go for a walk. He, like the others, was either trapped behind the walls of the checkpoint or out on patrol. None of them could nip down the pub for a pint.

'Dunno,' said Liam, not turning, maintaining his focus on the land in front of him, and the weapon in his hands. 'Just saying what I saw, that's all.'

'You really think he was going to slot you? Why the hell would he do that?'

'Clash of personalities,' Liam said, keeping their history private for now. 'It's not like the Army guarantees you'll like every soldier you have to work with, is it?'

'No kidding,' said Jackson, taking out a pouch of tobacco and some Rizlas. 'You don't smoke, do you?'

Liam shook his head.

'Sensible. Could kill you.'

Jackson finished making his rollie, then deftly flicked it into his mouth and lit it.

Watching Jackson take a draw, Liam was almost tempted to ask him to roll him one. He'd never smoked in his life, but for some reason, it seemed to fit with where they were, like another part of the uniform. And he could do with something to help him relax, even if it was a cigarette.

And it was then, as Liam breathed in the sweet, woody smell of Jackson's tobacco, that the RPG slammed into the wall right beneath where he was standing.

The walls shook, dust and grit and stone kicked up into the air and Liam instinctively dropped away and to the floor, half expecting it to give way beneath him.

He was given no time to think.

'Scott!' It was Corporal Jackson. 'Scott! Get on that bloody GPMG now! Return fire!'

Liam was up, readied the weapon, saw muzzle flash and unleashed a hail of metal as Jackson, eyes glued to the binos, tried to get eyes on where the RPG had come from.

A flash far off, about two hundred metres. Liam saw it clearly, realized it was nowhere near where he'd seen the muzzle flash and returned fire. Which meant there was more than one of them out there having a go.

Jackson yelled out, 'Incoming!'

The rocket landed short this time, but at least it had given away their enemy's position.

Liam was on it immediately, as was Mike from the

other lookout. The bush disappeared in a cloud of dust as the rounds smashed into it. Liam saw a shape moving to the left of where the RPG had been launched, tracked it with his weapon. He fired and the shape dropped from view – dead or just lucky, he didn't know.

Jackson was off the binos now and laying down fire with his own weapon. The rest of the lads were up on the wall and the peaceful evening disappeared quickly as the sound of gunfire shattered the gloom.

'Ten o'clock!' Liam yelled, jabbing a finger to the left of the checkpoint. 'Either they've moved or there's more of them!'

Jackson swung his weapon round and they both opened fire, but as soon as they did so, more rounds would come in but from another position. It was like shooting ghosts.

'This is stupid!' Liam yelled as more fire came in, this time from another position yet again. 'They're all over us! Where the crap are they?'

'Stop talking and keep at them!' Jackson shouted back, emptying his magazine and smoothly replacing it with a new one, like it was second nature, the weapon merely another part of his body.

A shout came up from below and Liam saw Cameron running towards them carrying a green tube.

'Here!' he shouted and passed it up to Liam. 'We've got about a dozen of these, I think.'

Liam took the tube. It was a Light Anti-Structures Missile (LASM), a 66mm unguided extendable rocket launcher, designed to be discarded after launch. Carrying a kilo of enhanced explosives, it used kinetic energy to penetrate the outer wall of the target structure, with the high-explosive warhead detonating inside. They were being phased out, to be replaced by the larger Anti-Structure Munition (ASM), but there were still enough around to be useful. As yet, Liam had only ever fired one on exercise. But things had just changed dramatically.

'You OK with that?' asked Jackson. 'Want me to do it?'

Liam shook his head, extending the launcher, the integral mechanical sight popping up automatically.

It was time to blow something up.

20

Liam placed the weapon on his right shoulder. It was light, and he thought how something with so much destructive power should really have weighed considerably more.

'Where are they?'

'To the left still,' said Corporal Jackson, letting out short, sharp bursts from his weapon to keep the shooters pinned down. 'Sustained fire is coming from the end of that field, where there's that section of crumbling mud wall. You see that?'

Liam trained the sight of the LASM on the place Jackson had described. 'Got it.'

'In your own time, Scott,' Jackson replied. 'So long as that's within the next five seconds and you give them a serious fucking headache.'

Liam let out a breath to steady himself.

'I'll keep their heads down,' said Jackson. 'Now

smash it, Scott, you hear me?' He continued to put down a good volley of suppressing fire.

Liam stared down the pop-up sight of the launcher. Calmly, he depressed the black switch on top of the green tubing and the rocket bucked out of the tube. A heartbeat later, Liam watched it slam into the section of old wall, which disintegrated immediately in a shower of old dry mud and brick. He knew that if anyone was behind it, there was no way they could have survived, or that there would be much of anything left.

Jackson opened fire once more and Liam joined in with the Gimpy, riddling the site with more bullets. Easing off, no fire was returned.

'Nice one, Scott,' said Jackson as Liam kicked the now-useless tube away so that they wouldn't trip over it.

But the battle was anything but over as more gunfire opened up on the checkpoint.

Jackson swore under his breath. 'I reckon we could be in for an all-nighter,' he said.

Liam didn't reply. He didn't have any words. All he had was an urge to make it through till dawn and to depend on his training. After all, in that moment, it was all he had. That, and the huge flood of adrenaline now racing through his body, and hard-wiring him to the battle they were now in.

Hours later, with midnight long gone, and dawn finally threatening to break through, Liam was dead on his feet. His legs didn't seem to work properly from either standing in one place too long and getting pins and needles, or having to maintain a semi-squatting position while firing the Gimpy. The Taliban hadn't let up all night, and no matter what Liam and the rest of the lads had thrown at them, they just seemed to keep coming back for more, taunting them almost. Liam had no idea how many kills, if any, they'd got, but it had clearly made sod all difference. And that was really pissing him off. It seemed that even a few dead mates wasn't enough to stop them.

'You need to get that seen to,' he said, nodding at Jackson, whose right cheek had been opened up with a deep gash. The blood had dried down his face, but the wound was still weeping.

'Nah, it's just a cut,' said Jackson, chugging down some water. 'Only a wood splinter, nothing to worry about. Gandalf can sort it later with his magical bag of medicine.' He passed the water to Liam. The gunfire had eased a little, but not completely, and sporadic rounds were being fired both into Checkpoint 3, and out.

'We've nearly twenty confirmed kills,' said Jackson. 'At least, that's how many I spotted through the binos

ANDY McNAB

before we ran out of flares. There could be more we just haven't seen.'

In the dark, and with no flares, the only thing they'd had to go on to pinpoint where the enemy fire was coming from was muzzle flash. But to Liam it seemed like they were trying to shoot at fireflies. They saw one, brought their arms to bear, and then another would pop up somewhere else. It was hopeless.

'It's making no difference,' he said. 'They just keep coming. Not even air support's stopped them.'

Sergeant Reynolds had called in three strikes that night, but even though each one had caused the battle to stall, the gunfire had soon started up again, often from a completely different location.

'They'll ease off when dawn breaks,' said Jackson. 'Without the cover of darkness, they'll scuttle off to whatever cave it is they've been planning this attack from.'

'And what? Wait it out?'

Liam didn't like where his thoughts were leading. Because if the Taliban came back for more, then the multiple would get to a point where they had nothing left to throw back but rocks. Then what?

'Just have to wait and see, Scott,' said Jackson. 'And try not to get killed.'

*   *   *

184

When dawn did break, and the day peeked over the horizon as though nervous of what it would see, Reynolds got the lads to do a stocktake. By lunch time, everyone was jittery. Come evening, Liam knew there was a real possibility of things not coming good for any of them.

'So what you're saying,' said Reynolds, the lads sitting around him, though he was now staring hard at Corporal Jackson, who'd been in charge of tallying everything up, 'is that we've not got enough to get us through another night like the one we just had.'

'Pretty much,' said Jackson with a shrug. 'So unless you want us fixing bayonets and doing a re-enactment of Rorke's Drift, we need to either get the hell out of here, or be re-supplied immediately.'

'Sounds like we're fucked,' said Jason.

'Can it!' snapped Reynolds. 'We are not fucked and we are not going to be fucked, so you can bin that attitude immediately.'

Jason nodded, but said nothing more as Reynolds ordered John onto the radio. Connection made, he took the receiver, the conversation punctuated by well-delivered swearing and a hell of a lot of shouting.

'The short answer,' he said, looking at the lads as he hung up the radio, slamming it home like he wanted it to break, 'is that we're stuck here. That is, until someone can pull enough of his or her head out of their arse to see that we're in the shit up to our eyeballs and send a cow in to pick us up.'

'No way will they send a Chinook out,' said Jason. 'Terry would knock it out of the sky in a minute. Ground's too hot. We don't know how many are out there, if there are more coming in. Nothing.'

'Sodding typical,' said Corporal Jackson. 'Being quiet for weeks and nothing's been sent because no one thought we needed it. Now we do, it's too dangerous. Genius.'

'So they're doing a drop,' continued Reynolds as Jason's voice died to a mumbling grumble. 'Cover of darkness, so it's a tough call. Not easy to accurately throw something out of an aircraft in the middle of the night. But it's the best chance we've got. They're doing the fly-by at 2100 hours. So keep your eyes on the skies for a crate of stuff coming our way.'

When the time came, Liam heard the distant telltale sound of an aeroplane.

'Here she comes,' said Cameron, who was standing with him. 'Santa on a C130.'

The plane passed overhead and Liam was just about able to make out its silhouette against the night sky. But his eyes were looking for something else, and when it exploded out above them, catching air as it plummeted

– a parachute carrying with it a crate of supplies – he joined in with the others and cheered.

Liam, Cameron, Paul and John were ready at the gate of the checkpoint to head out and drag the supplies back in, fully expecting the package to drop, as promised, pretty much at their front door. Except it didn't.

'It's drifting!' called Mike, who was up in the sangar again. 'God knows how, seeing as there's no sodding wind at all, but it's drifting badly.'

Everyone looked up. Liam saw it and Mike was right. It was going to miss them completely.

'Brilliant,' said Jason as the parachute disappeared from view behind trees and scrubland about a mile away. 'All they've done is gone and resupplied the Taliban. Given them extra stuff to kill us with. What a total fuck-up.'

'We're screwed,' said Cameron.

'Pretty much,' agreed Liam.

Reynolds quickly pulled them all together. 'This is the situation,' he said, and Liam had never seen or heard him so serious. 'If it kicks off tonight like it did last night, there's a good chance we'll be overrun.'

'How do you mean?' asked Liam. 'What, they'll try to get in?'

'There's no *try* about it,' said Jackson. 'If we've got nothing to throw back at them, they'll want to be in here for us, simple as that. And believe me, they'll fucking well succeed too.'

Liam went cold. What he was hearing couldn't be true. But it was. Every soldier's worst nightmare – to be overrun and taken prisoner. Except here the Geneva Convention wasn't exactly bedtime reading, and prisoners of war weren't even used as bargaining tools. They were propaganda. And in the eyes of the Taliban, the bloodier the better.

'Everyone,' said Sergeant Reynolds, keeping order, 'is to destroy all possible forms of identification. And by that I mean all letters, name tags, absolutely anything that can trace you or give away any information about who you are and where you're from. All of it must be destroyed.'

He paused, composing himself.

'I'm not going to bullshit you. You must all of you ready yourselves for the possibility of capture and all that it would entail. I don't need to go into any more detail than that, I'm sure; you all know it.'

Sergeant Reynolds let out a breath, then stared at the soldiers in turn.

'Suffice to say, lads,' he growled, 'this is our party and they're not invited, so let's make absolutely fucking sure we don't let the bastards in.'

Jackson shouted over to Liam. 'Muzzle flash to the right, mate! Get some stuck in there!'

Liam swung his aim and squeezed the trigger. A hellish hail of metal blasted out from the GPMG, destroying the section of bush that Jackson had directed him to. Then, just when he thought that nothing could get up from the ferocious spray of bullets he'd fired, the area lit up with the telltale flash of a rocket.

'RPG!' he screamed. 'RPG! Incoming!'

Liam had lost count of just how many he'd seen fired at them since heading out from Camp Bastion. But it didn't make this one any less deadly. Unable to move, and frozen for a moment by what approached, Liam just stood and stared as the rocket blasted towards the compound. Hands grabbed him, tried to pull him to the ground, but he couldn't move. It was like he was hypnotized by the sight of the fire and flame and heat spitting out behind the rocket. Then it slammed with brutal effectiveness into Cameron and Mike's sangar at a speed touching 300 metres per second. Only this rocket was luckier than the one that had come at him and Jackson. Instead of impacting almost uselessly on the wall just below, it skipped in through the opening Mike and Cameron had been firing from – and took it apart.

The roof of the lookout shot up in the air, then glided back through the night to the ground, like a leaf falling from a giant tree. Dust and muck and metal and wood burst outwards, a deadly spray of violent shrapnel capable of ripping to pieces anything in its way.

A moment after the impact Liam made to drop to his knees, but was too late, and the shockwave bashed into him, knocking him back into Jackson. They both crashed to the ground, their weapons clattering about them. Liam crunched his head on the spent tube of the launcher he'd used earlier, and the pain of the impact was like someone hammering a six-inch nail into his head.

Dazed, but on autopilot now, Liam was up and out of the sangar, grabbing a medical kit on the way and racing across the stony courtyard of the checkpoint. From the corner of his eye he saw Jackson get up, make to follow him, then get back onto the GPMG and open fire. As he ran, bits and pieces of Cameron and Mike's sangar rained down about him, falling to the ground like confetti.

Liam caught sight of John, Jason and Paul, all turning to join in and search for their mates, but Sergeant Reynolds had all of them bar Paul back at their posts.

'Back on your weapons and keep their heads down!' he barked. 'Or shoot them off, I don't care which! Gandalf – you're needed!'

Climbing up to the sangar, Liam found that his

vision was obscured by the dense cloud of dust swirling around in the air. It got into his eyes, made them water, and he put his hand over his mouth to stop it choking him. The smell of it was worse than usual. Not just the dry dust, explosives and burning, but something sweet was in there too, and he knew it was the reek of burned, scorched flesh.

'Dinsdale! Where the hell are you? Dinsdale! Fucking well answer me!'

No answer came and when Liam reached where Cameron and Mike had been standing, he saw why.

The place itself was rubble and ruin. Sand and grit and rock were strewn everywhere. With the force of the explosion, wood and slivers of metal from the roof had embedded themselves in the walls and the floor.

Liam started to call out again, but then spotted something. Whether it was Mike or Cameron he wasn't at first sure. It was just the top of someone's head, matted with dust and dirt and blood. He looked around, could see no one else lying in front of him. Climbing up, Liam saw that the rest of the body was, as far as he could tell, covered in the shattered, broken remains of the sangar. It was only on edging closer that he realized it was Cameron.

Or what was left of him.

Both of Cameron's legs had been blown off at the

knee, the mashed-up stumps a mess of torn flesh and bone, blood thick with muck and dirt. The right side of Cameron's body was a mess of weeping burns and dust, all mixing up into a thick, oily mud. The Kevlar plates in his body armour had obviously protected him a little, but they were twisted and broken, and Liam could see nasty jagged splinters of wood jutting out from his sides, from his arms. Cameron's face was burned and cut and bloodied.

The shock of what was now before him hammered down onto Liam and he had to stop himself collapsing. For a moment, though, he couldn't move, the utter appalling horror flooring him immediately.

Paul appeared as Liam stalled, nailed to the moment by the murderous violence in front of him.

'Hacker was blown out of the lookout!' he shouted. 'The hard bastard's somehow survived!'

Liam heard what Paul said, but he wasn't really listening. Dropping to his knees, he dragged all that he knew about first aid from the back of his mind, pushed it forwards, and got on with what he knew he had to do: clean Cameron down, and try and save his life. Paul joined him as he pulled a tourniquet out of the medical kit and tightened it around Cameron's left leg. Cameron shuddered, his breathing ragged and rattling in his throat.

'I need another tourniquet! Now!'

Paul was on it even as Liam's words died and he took over and dealt with Cameron's right leg immediately with lightning proficiency.

'Speak to him!' Paul shouted at Liam, as he began to sort out the rest of Cameron's appalling injuries. 'Remember your training. He knows you best out of the lot of us, so it's you he needs now. I can deal with his injuries.'

Paul then shouted down to Sergeant Reynolds, who Liam saw was on the radio immediately and calling in a medevac.

Liam grabbed Cameron's hand. 'Dinsdale, it's Scott,' he said, not really knowing what to say to someone in such a state. He'd never seen anything like this before, and if he'd expected his emotions to go crazy, the exact opposite had happened: if anything, he felt numb, dead almost. 'Gandalf's dealing with your injuries and Sergeant Reynolds has called for a medevac. You're going to be fine, just stick with me, OK? I'm not leaving your side. Just hold on.'

Another explosion shook the compound.

'The bastards won't give up now!' hissed Paul under his breath.

Liam spoke again to Cameron. 'You're going to owe me after this, mate,' he said. 'And I don't mean a few beers either. My cleaning bill's going to be massive, thanks to you.'

'You're doing good,' said Paul. 'Keep it up, OK? Even if he's not responding, just keep on reassuring him. He just needs to hear your voice.'

Liam did exactly that, and was soon talking about Jon and Matt, reminiscing about their training.

Sergeant Reynolds appeared. 'Medevac's on its way,' he said. 'As cover we've got three Apache helicopters heading our way to pummel Terry with a shitload of ordnance.'

The Apache, armed with an M230 chain gun, Hellfire missiles and flechette-armed rockets, was a weapon Liam knew the Taliban were seriously afraid of. The chain gun alone was capable of unleashing a hail of exploding shells, with a kill radius of 10 feet when used against unprotected, standing targets, at 300 rpm. The Hellfire missile was a laser-guided weapon carrying a twenty-pound warhead, accurate to a range of 8,000 metres and effective against tanks and pretty much anything else it was thrown at. The flechette-armed rockets would send in a cloud of over 80 5-inch-long darts travelling at Mach 1, and capable of piercing tree trunks.

'There's also a C130 gunship in the air, so it's doing a fly-by for us,' added the sergeant. 'It's closing in to give the Taliban a good hammering before the Apache get here to clean up what's left. It's going to get noisy.'

'They're sending a Spectre gunship?' said Paul, raising a grim smile. 'Then it's bye-bye Taliban.'

'Is he going to make it?' Liam said, looking at the sergeant and forgetting his training for a second, his concern for the life of his friend overriding everything else. Paul had already sorted Cameron as best he could, stabilized him, and bandaged his wounds.

'I'll come for you when the medevac arrives,' said Sergeant Reynolds, not answering Liam's question. 'Between now and then, keep your head down, cover your ears and talk to Cameron. Understand?'

'Yes, Sergeant.' Liam nodded, and Reynolds was gone.

A few minutes later the whole world shook like an earthquake had hit.

'That'll be the gunship,' said Paul. 'Be thankful we're not on the receiving end of what it's sending down.'

Liam knew exactly what Paul was getting at. Armed with two 20mm M61 Vulcan cannons, one Bofors 40mm autocannon, and one 105mm M102 cannon, the gunship could saturate a target with an almost un-matchable amount of firepower. It was as horrifying as it was awesome. There was no surviving what it could spit out if you got in its way.

The sound died down. Then, as Liam was continuing to chatter on to Cameron, the darkness was split apart by the white light of explosions ripping apart the Taliban positions.

'That's the Apache,' said Paul. 'Whatever wasn't dead to begin with soon will be. You ready?'

Liam nodded. Then Sergeant Reynolds' voice cut through the moment. 'Medevac's a minute away!'

The minute went by in a second, and with Liam and Jackson's help, the rescue crew had Cameron strapped onto a stretcher, wired into a saline drip and out of the ruins of the sangar.

In the courtyard of the compound, Sergeant Reynolds ordered the multiple to cover the extraction.

'I'll go with Dinsdale,' said Liam, making ready to head off with the rescue team. 'I need to.'

Reynolds, however, ordered him back up into the remaining sangar with Jackson.

'He's got the best chance he'll ever have now that the medevac's here,' he explained. 'You've still got a job to do. Now let them do theirs.'

'But he's my mate!' said Liam; and he knew how weak he sounded, but no other words would come. All he could see was his injured mate and he'd never in his life felt as helpless as he did at that moment.

'You've done all you can, Scott,' said Reynolds,

stepping closer, his voice firm yet kind. 'Let the pros take over.'

Liam glanced up at his sergeant. The man looked weary, covered in dust, but there remained a steel in his eyes that betrayed his fierce determination not to let the Taliban have their day. 'Your job is to man your weapon and make sure that any Taliban lucky enough to have survived that assault from the air are occupied enough to ignore the helicopter.'

Liam watched as Cameron was stretchered towards the waiting Chinook; then, with a nod from Sergeant Reynolds, he jogged back to the surviving sangar. The sound of the Chinook lifting off seemed to rattle the darkness, and Liam, back on the GPMG, opened fire on what was left of the Taliban, his fury at what had happened to Cameron raw and burning and hungry for revenge.

22

When morning slipped forward from the horizon, a stillness hung in the air, as did the smell of a firefight. Liam was exhausted, but still too gunned up to rest. Leaning against the GPMG, his eyes staring into the light, willing the Taliban to show themselves, he tried to ignore the images burned into his mind of Cameron and his injuries. It didn't work. Even when he closed his eyes, he saw them.

Sergeant Reynolds gave a call for the multiple to come together. Liam and Corporal Jackson ducked out of their sangar and came down into the compound. Sergeant Reynolds was sitting round where they usually met to discuss foot patrols. John, Paul, Jason and Mike were with him.

Liam stared at Mike as he sat down. The man was bruised, his clothes torn, but that was about it. He looked hardly any different. How the hell had he survived?

With everyone quiet, Sergeant Reynolds started to speak, his face serious and drained of all colour.

'Dinsdale was immediately taken to surgery on arrival at Camp Bastion,' he said, his voice stating each word in a tone that seemed to be working almost too hard to display no emotion. 'However, after two hours with the surgeons, he . . .' Sergeant Reynolds stumbled over his words. Liam's whole body froze. He didn't want to hear what the sergeant was going to say next, but there was nothing he could do to stop it. 'His injuries were just too severe,' he went on. 'Dinsdale died at just after 0400 hours.'

'Scott?'

Liam, his eyes still stinging with tears, looked up into the face of Sergeant Reynolds.

'We need to sort Dinsdale's stuff out,' said the sergeant. 'It has to be done now, in case something else kicks off. We owe it to him. And because you knew him better than the rest of us, you're the one best suited to making sure everything that *should* go home *does*.'

Liam understood. 'I'll do it now,' he said, and stood up. His muscles were so tight it was as though they might snap with even the smallest of movements.

'You did everything you could,' said Sergeant Reynolds. 'You must know that.'

Liam nodded weakly, forced back the tears that threatened to bubble up again.

'I've lost mates,' said the sergeant, his voice lower, a little more friendly perhaps, but no less authoritative. 'But there's a time and a place to deal with the grief. You're a good soldier, Scott. Focus on that. Don't let what happened cause you to lose focus and drop your guard. I'm depending on you as much as the others.'

With that, Sergeant Reynolds left and Liam made his way over to Cameron's bed. Sitting down, he slumped forward, dropping his head into his hands. He was numb, like the death of Cameron had taken away all feeling, all sensation. He wanted to cry, but couldn't. What tears he'd shed had already dried up. Nothing seemed to work inside him to make sense of what had happened. But that was the problem, wasn't it? There was no sense in it. No reason. They were in a war zone. People got killed. It could just as easily have been any of them, but this time it was Cameron.

Liam sat back, stared at the sky. He'd lost two friends now. First Dan, now Cameron. He wanted to be any-where but here. Cameron was the one constant he'd had through training and out to Afghanistan, and Liam had never felt so alone in his life. Or so helpless. Then he thought about what the sergeant had said and knew that he was right. He had a loyalty not just to Cameron's memory but to his mates; hell, even to Mike. He'd grieve for Cameron later, and do it properly. If he dwelled on it now, he'd only be letting the Taliban win. And he wasn't about to let that happen.

A few minutes later, as Liam was just finishing the hard task of sorting through Cameron's stuff, a shout came from across the compound and he snapped round to see Lance Corporal Jackson signalling for everyone to join him. With nothing else to do for Cameron, Liam jogged over, arriving at the same time as Mike. Neither of them looked at each other, or said a word. When everyone was together, Sergeant Reynolds told them what the fuss was all about.

'We've just this moment received the emergency code *Man Away*,' he said. 'A lad from the multiple at Checkpoint 1 has gone missing.'

Liam saw Jason sign for everyone to stop. With Cameron's death not even twelve hours gone, and now away from Checkpoint 3 and searching for a lost soldier, Liam was raging inside. He wasn't just out here on a manhunt. He was out to get one back on the Taliban for killing his friend.

With Macdonald, Pearce, White and Allan restocked with fresh supplies of ammunition, Liam and the rest were picked up in a Chinook and flown to where the missing soldier had last been seen. Though it was an area they'd not covered before, it looked no different to the area of Afghanistan he'd grown used to. Strangely, he longed to be back home and walking through a little bit of rain. Afghanistan's endless dryness and dust-filled air was something he figured he would never miss.

According to what Sergeant Reynolds had said, pretty much every Coalition soldier within a hundred-mile radius had been sent in to join with the search. A missing soldier was a priority above all others. After all, if you went missing yourself, you'd want to think the rest of the Army was turning the country upside down to find you. And, right at that moment, that was exactly what it was doing.

Jason pointed. 'Pile of stones up ahead,' he said. 'Looks bloody suspicious, if you ask me. Just going to take a look.'

Liam wanted him to get a move on, but that wasn't about to happen. Any possible hint of an IED was caution city: there was no point hurrying and getting blown apart. In front of him, Liam saw Mike shifting from one foot to another, keeping his blood flowing to stop them going numb, but at that moment, whatever Mike thought of him, he could not have cared less. All that mattered was soldiering. It was something he was good at and he wasn't going to fuck up.

Liam looked ahead to see Jason stretched out on his belly, slowly prising apart an odd little pile of stones with a thin length of metal. From where Liam was he could see that Jason had been right: the stones did look strange.

A moment later, Jason called out 'Clear!' then climbed back to his feet. The multiple moved off again, treading in his footsteps along the track they'd been following for the past half a mile.

Liam did his best to ignore the flashbacks to Cameron's injuries, but it was near impossible. After a while, he just accepted them and used the feelings to make him even more alert. The track was narrow, barely wide enough to walk two abreast, and Liam just couldn't work out what its purpose could ever have been. It didn't connect anything to something else, and though worn, there were few signs, if any, that anyone had used it in the last thousand years. It was just a simple track, probably of no use to anything but a few goats.

He turned his attention to the fields running down their left. They'd been harvested and were lying bare for the sun to bake them up. A series of channels and gullies and ditches divided the fields from each other, and most had water flowing in the bottom, turning the earth to a thick, sticky gloop.

Liam had found from experience that the longer he

stared at the view, the less he saw. So he did what he always did when this happened. He closed his eyes, took a breath to focus, then opened them again. It took a moment for his eyes to recalibrate, but when they did, something leaped out at him. It was an odd shape lying in a field. Its outline was soft, rather than lumpy and jagged as it would have been were it comprised of stones and lumps of mud. He stared at it a bit longer. No, there was definitely something wrong here. Whatever it was, it didn't belong, and they needed to have a nosy.

'Sergeant!'

Reynolds snapped round. 'What is it, Scott?'

Liam pointed out into the field. 'Over there. Don't know what it is, but it doesn't look right.'

Sergeant Reynolds grabbed his binos and the rest of the multiple swung their eyes to where Liam was looking.

Seconds passed slow and steady, like honey running off a spoon.

'Call it in!' shouted Sergeant Reynolds to Jackson, who was already on the radio. 'We've found him.'

Liam, not thinking, made to step forward.

'Don't bloody move!' yelled the corporal.

Liam froze.

'The ground in front of us isn't clear,' Jackson continued. 'Could be anything out there. Think!'

There was a moment's silence.

'Right,' said Reynolds. 'Everyone back to me. Now.'

The soldiers gathered around the sergeant.

'OK, listen in. We've found him. But we have no idea what state he's in, if he's injured, dead, even booby-trapped.'

That thought made Liam sick to his gut – that anyone would use another human being as a trap. But he knew that it happened, and Sergeant Reynolds had been right to hold them back.

'Finch,' ordered the sergeant, 'I want you going in. Standard procedure, but be more cautious than ever, right?'

Jason nodded.

'The rest of you, I want eyes on the surrounding area. Anything moves, anything so much as breathes, we need to identify it and make sure it's a friendly. If it isn't, we take it out. And we need Finch covered. Anything kicks off then we get him back here sharp. Understood?'

Everyone nodded a 'Yes, Sergeant.'

Jason moved off and the rest of the multiple spread out. Liam scanned the surrounding area, but the brush was thick, impenetrable, and if anyone was hiding out there, he had a horrible feeling they wouldn't know until the bullets went flying. He flicked his eyes to Jason. He was halfway to the downed soldier, going slow, checking everything. One casualty was bad, but two would be a hell of a lot worse.

Jason was at the soldier now, checking him over, going slow, methodical with every movement he made. He turned his head towards the others and raised a hand. Liam wasn't sure what he meant. Was the soldier OK, dead, what? He looked past Mike, who was on his knees some twenty metres on, and over to Sergeant Reynolds for confirmation of what they were doing next.

The crack of a gunshot split the moment. Liam turned, saw Jason drop to the ground.

'Man down!' yelled Jackson. 'Man down!'

But Jason was up again, returning fire.

'Cover him!' shouted Sergeant Reynolds. 'Now!'

Bullets flew as Liam and the rest opened up with everything they had. The sound of automatic weapons danced in the air. Liam saw Jason grab the downed soldier, hoist him over his shoulders, then leg it back towards them. The multiple put down a solid wall of fire as Jason, his legs hammering hard, his face stern and determined, raced towards them. When he reached Sergeant Reynolds, he skidded to the ground.

The way the soldier's body fell from Jason's shoulders, Liam knew he was dead. That, and the dark stains he could see on his clothing, a clear sign that the body was riddled with bullets. Anger bubbled inside him, boiled over.

Liam emptied his magazine and changed it quick and sharp, hurling out another spray of bullets. Along from him, the rest of the multiple did the same. Then he saw a hand signal from Sergeant Reynolds. They were pulling out. He wanted to stay, to take the fight to the Taliban – to the ones who'd killed Cameron, killed the soldier they'd come out here to find – but he knew the sergeant was right.

'Mike!' Liam yelled. 'Hacker! We need to shift it!'

Mike nodded and they both stood up, making to move up to the others; then more fire came in at them, this time from another position. Suddenly the ground between them and Sergeant Reynolds and the other soldiers was kicked up into the air and a dull thud hammered both of them onto the ground.

'Mortar rounds!' Mike yelled out. 'They've cut us off! We have to get the fuck out of here!'

'I know that!' Liam shouted back and pointed towards Sergeant Reynolds. 'That way!'

Another mortar round came in, closer this time, quickly followed by another.

Mike zipped a finger across his throat. 'No way, Liam! They've got our position. We go that way, they'll blow us to pieces or just mow us down. Now shift it!' He pointed behind Liam.

'But that's the wrong direction!'

'We'll swing round,' said Mike, nodding back to the direction the others were going in. 'No choice. Fire, manoeuvre, OK? Move!'

Liam didn't argue, wasn't given a chance, as Mike pushed him to his feet and opened fire. Liam bolted, sprinting hard. After about ten metres, he turned, dropped to his knees, opened fire. Mike was up, sprinted past, and between five and ten metres further on did the same, covering Liam as he moved.

Liam dropped down into a gully, his lungs bursting, sweat pouring down his face. Mike joined him.

'Where the hell are we going?'

'At this moment,' said Mike, 'away from that lot. If we'd stayed we'd have been torn apart. But we can't stay here. We need to keep moving and get back to the others.' He crept to the top of the gully, peered over. The sound of gunfire opened up. 'They're on to us,' he confirmed. 'We can't stay here. How are you for ammo?'

Liam checked. He was down two mags, but the other ten he was carrying were fine. That gave him a total of 300 rounds, along with some grenades in his pack.

'We've enough between us to get out of this,' said Mike. 'But we're going to have to keep moving or they'll be on to us. And we're just going to have to hope that wherever we're going is IED-free, because we can't afford to go creeping around. Understand?'

Liam nodded. He was scared, but if he was honest he would have been more worried if he hadn't been. Fear, he knew now, gave a soldier an edge, kept him alert. And being shot at by the Taliban, and now being paired up with Mike, was more than reason enough, as Jackson sometimes said, his tongue firmly in his cheek, 'to stay frosty'.

'We stick to the drills, Liam,' said Mike. 'Use our training. Let's move!'

Liam followed him down the gully and it wasn't long before his sense of direction was screwed. The sound of gunfire, though quieter, was still following them and he knew that they could very soon become the focus of a search-and-rescue operation themselves, just like the one they were supposed to be on right now.

Mike pointed skywards. 'Evening's drawing in. We don't want to be stuck out here longer than we have to.' He nodded to his right. 'The others will be making their way back to where we were dropped off. Which, if I'm right, is that way.'

'So what are you suggesting?' asked Liam, his hands gripping his SA80, not just because he was ready for the Taliban, but because he was wary of Mike.

'We've no choice but to hit open ground,' said Mike. 'How fast can you run?'

'Faster than you,' said Liam.

'Then let's see, shall we?'

Liam and Mike checked over the lip of the gully, peering through the bushes to see if anyone had sussed them yet. The landscape was flat and dusty – the usual series of fields, most dry and barren, bordered by rough scrub, ditches and badly maintained paths and roads. In the distance, mountains rose to stare down on them.

'We're clear,' said Mike, and he was up and out of the gully.

Liam leaped out after him. Mike was powerfully built and could run, but Liam was quick, always had been, and soon he was alongside.

Gunfire came at them, kicking up dust to their sides. Mike changed direction and dropped behind a large tree. Liam skidded in next to him. Without a word, they both readied their weapons.

'Thought you said we were clear?' hissed Liam.

'I was wrong,' Mike replied. 'Sue me.'

Peering round the tree, Liam spotted four men approaching from the way they'd just come. They were all carrying AK47s and firing wildly from the hip in their general direction. Liam raised his rifle.

'Wait,' said Mike, his hand lowering Liam's weapon.

'We don't waste rounds. Every shot has to count. Hold till they're almost on us. You take those two on the right, I'll have the ones on the left.'

Liam nodded.

The men still approached. They were shouting now, and they sounded happy, like they were already sure of their kill. Liam could hear the blood thumping through his head, racing around his body. Any closer and he'd be able to hug them.

'*Now!*' hissed Mike.

Liam was up, had the first man in his sights, squeezed the trigger, dropping him to the ground like a rag doll with a three-round burst. He switched to the other, squeezed the trigger again, gave another three-round blast and dropped him too. Then he turned to the others to find that neither one was standing.

'Move!' shouted Mike, and pushed Liam to take point.

Liam leaped out from their firing position behind the tree and raced on. He turned, dropped to his knees to provide covering fire for Mike, but there was no one coming for them, no gunfire. Perhaps they were in the clear?

Mike bolted past and Liam was up and chasing. Ahead, he saw a tumbledown compound. One of the walls had fallen in completely. It wasn't much, but it would give them some cover and a chance to work out what to do next. Liam leaped over the fallen wall and dropped against the part of it still standing. He checked his weapon, made sure that if anyone came after them, he was still ready to go.

Mike arrived. But he didn't sit down.

'I don't think any others are coming after us,' he said.

'That was insane,' said Liam, and pulled out his water bottle to take a deep glug. He threw it to Mike, who caught it, but didn't take a drink.

'How you doing, Liam?' Mike placed the bottle on the ground.

'Oh, I'm just peachy,' said Liam, laughing to himself at the thought that now, of all times, he was using a phrase of his mum's.

'I mean about Cameron's death,' said Mike. 'It must've hit you hard.'

'I don't want to talk about it,' said Liam, and he really didn't, particularly not with Mike. 'I just want to get back to the checkpoint.'

'But what if *I* want to talk about it?' said Mike, and Liam heard the change in his voice. Before, it had been urgent, but calm and focused on getting them away from the Taliban. Now it was cold and direct. Angry.

'Why?' asked Liam. 'It's not as though you knew him that well, is it?'

Liam didn't like this. Mike was rounding on him.

'It's hard, though, isn't it?' said Mike, turning away from Liam. 'When someone close to you dies. Tough to deal with. Like it was for my family when you got Dan killed.'

Liam found it hard to believe what Mike was doing, what he was saying.

'I didn't get Dan killed,' he said, trying not to raise his voice, anger Mike further. 'It was an accident! He tripped. I tried to catch him, but—'

'But nothing, Liam!' Mike snarled. 'Dan's death destroyed my family! *You* destroyed my family!'

Liam heard a sound any soldier would recognize: a weapon being readied. It was Mike's SA80. He slid back the cocking handle on his own, just in case.

Mike hurled himself round, weapon at the ready and pointed directly at Liam's chest.

'You killed my brother, Liam!'

'No I didn't!' Liam yelled back, his barrel now trained on Mike's chest. 'And whatever you're thinking of doing now, don't do it! This isn't what either of us want! Don't be a fucking idiot!'

'I know what I know,' hissed Mike. 'It was your fault, Liam. Dan's dead because of you.'

He raised the barrel of his rifle . . .

23

Liam hurled his right hand towards Mike, launching a cloud of dust and grit into his face. Mike, caught by surprise, ducked, but at the same time squeezed off a few rounds from his SA80. They thumped into the wall above where Liam had been sitting, but now Liam was up on his feet and more pissed off than he'd ever been in his whole life.

'You stupid fuck!' he yelled. 'You tried to bloody well slot me!'

He didn't give Mike a chance to reply, slamming his whole body into him to knock him to the ground. Mike struggled, but his eyes were still filled with grit. He swiped at Liam with his weapon, but Liam slapped him hard across his face with the back of his hand, then knelt on his right arm, which was holding the SA80. Mike yelled out, but Liam only leaned on it harder, grinding it into the ground.

Mike's hand sprang open, dropping the rifle. Liam grabbed it and hurled it away. But now Mike could see exactly what he was doing and he caught Liam hard across the jaw, sending him onto his side.

Liam tried to get up, but Mike was into him hard with a boot. Liam curled up, protecting himself from the kick. Mike came in again, but Liam managed to roll out of his way and was up on his feet again.

'Back off, Mike!' he shouted. 'Don't be such an idiot! I didn't kill Dan!'

'You were there!' snarled Mike, wiping more muck from his face. 'If it hadn't been for you, he wouldn't have been there in the first place. My brother, he looked up to you. Fuck knows why, but he did. And you encouraged him, didn't you? Got him into trouble when he should've been home studying, sorting a life for himself.'

Liam saw Mike eye his rifle, but it was too far away. Then he went for his pistol.

Liam had no choice. Instead of turning to run, he killed the distance between them in a snap. As Mike raised the pistol, Liam grabbed the hand holding the weapon and pushed it hard and fast into Mike's gut. Then, giving Mike no quarter, he launched a flurry of ferociously violent punches into his face, smashing his nose in a spray of blood and splitting an eyebrow open. Liam gave no thought to the fact that he could easily break his fingers. At that moment it didn't matter. With Mike's nose now broken, blood pouring down his face, Liam turned his attention to the pistol, grabbing it with both hands and tearing it away from Mike with a terrible yank.

Mike yelled out and Liam knew immediately that he'd just broken his trigger finger.

He raised the weapon. 'Stand still!' he screamed at Mike. 'Don't move! Just stay the fuck where you are!'

But Mike wasn't listening. 'I'm going to kill you, Liam.'

'Just stay where you are, you mad bastard!'

'I mean it,' continued Mike. 'You're dead, Liam. Fucking dead!'

Liam didn't know what to do next. They couldn't stay here for ever, facing each other down. And he wasn't about to put a bullet in Mike to slow him down. It was tempting, but it was stupid. Despite what the movies portrayed, Liam knew it was nigh on impossible to wound someone on purpose. One shot and Mike would most likely end up bleeding to death.

'What you going to do now then, Liam?' Mike asked, wiping blood and snot from his face. 'You know you're going to have to shoot me, don't you? Come on then! Do it! Because if you don't, I'm going to—'

Whatever Mike was going to say was cut short by the

sight of a grenade landing on the ground to their left. They both jumped for their lives, Liam diving behind the remains of the destroyed wall, Mike dropping behind a pile of stones.

The grenade went off, filling the place with smoke. Liam heard shrapnel ping all around, and when he opened his eyes, he could see nothing. There was no sound from Mike. Liam found himself hoping he was at least injured, but binned that thought immediately when he saw his silhouette, about thirty metres away, scrabbling around in the dust for his rifle.

Liam was up and out of the compound in a breath. He made to grab his rifle, but the thing had been caught in the blast and was a mess, smashed up and crushed by flying debris. Where he was going he wasn't sure, but out of there was his first thought – away from Mike, who he had no doubt was still intent on murdering him; and away from the Taliban, who had obviously found where they were hiding and tossed in the grenade to wake them up.

Liam heard gunfire but didn't turn round. Then he heard Mike shouting after him, but he ignored it and just kept running.

The evening was almost over now, and night was only minutes away. Soon the whole area would be dark. And dark in the desert of Afghanistan was dark – nothing like the gloom of a city, but a sheer impenetrable blackness lit only by the stars. Liam knew he couldn't go wandering around, unable to see where he was going; he had to find somewhere to hide up for the night. But where?

He spotted some thick bush about a hundred metres ahead, a small area of woodland with trees and scrub and rubble. It would do, but only if no one saw him. He dropped to the ground, calmed his breath, listened out. Silence. Slowly he edged forward. Then, just ahead, he spotted something. He was on a narrow path, and a few metres in front of him an area of ground had been scuffed up, but in a different direction to any other mark he could see. It looked like it had been swept by a branch to cover something up. Liam knew that if Jason were here he'd have stopped the multiple and gone to investigate. For all he knew, it was nothing, just a patch of ground where a goat had taken a kip. But he wasn't about to take that risk. So he stepped round it, giving the area a wide berth.

'Liam!'

It was Mike, and he was closing in.

Liam knew that with Mike so near, the small woodland was now binned – he'd have to find somewhere else. Where? He edged forward, scanning the area ahead, hoping Mike would just give up and back off. Some chance, he thought.

The thump of an explosion pulled Liam up sharp. For a moment, there was silence, then there was a sickening moan.

Liam turned back the way he'd come and knew what he was going to find even before he stumbled on it. A few steps later, and in the half-light cast by the moon, he saw Mike sprawled on the ground. His right foot was gone, bits of it scattered in the bushes and across the ground.

To his amazement, he saw Mike sit up and raise his weapon.

'You're injured, Mike!' said Liam. 'Don't be such a prick!'

But the weapon went off and Liam heard a bullet whistle past his head. Then Mike's arm dropped to the ground, weakness taking over.

Liam ran over and kicked the rifle out of the way. Then he knelt down at Mike's side and removed his knife. 'You can try and kill me later,' he said. 'Now, though, we have to sort out this mess.'

He started to check Mike over for further injuries, but Mike snarled and attempted to land a punch on his cheek. It missed badly. He tried again, but this time Liam grabbed him tight, leaning his arm across Mike's neck to choke him.

'You've a choice, Mike,' he hissed, spitting angrily. 'Either back down and give me a chance to sort you out, or fuck around and have me walk away.'

Mike glared.

'Believe me,' said Liam, 'I'm seriously tempted to leave you here to bleed to death or be captured by the Taliban.' Mike's eyes grew wide and Liam sensed his body relax beneath him. 'Your foot's gone,' Liam continued. 'But you don't seem to have any other injuries. Must've been a small device. However, I still need to stop the bleeding, clean you up and get you out of here. Understand?'

Mike nodded feebly.

'Good,' said Liam. 'Now keep quiet. And if you hear anything, tell me!'

With Mike quickly subdued, not just because of blood loss and exhaustion, but the shot of morphine to dull the pain, Liam dealt with Mike's injuries. A tourniquet stemmed the bleeding and, once the wound was as clean as he could make it with the water from his pack, he had it packed and bandaged in minutes.

'Liam . . . voices . . .'

Mike's voice was barely a whisper, but what it said was enough to silence Liam.

Mike was right: there *were* voices. Distant, but

distinct, and Liam recognized only the sound of locals, not squaddies.

He leaned in close for Mike to hear him. 'We have to get out of here,' he said. 'And that means I'm going to have to carry you.'

Mike said nothing, just nodded.

'You're going on my shoulders, fireman's carry, but I need you to make like you're dead and keep your mouth shut. Even if it hurts like hell, don't make a sound or we're screwed.'

Mike made no effort to contradict what Liam had said. Once Liam was happy that he could carry his kit and Mike's SA80 securely, he helped Mike up onto his good foot, ducked down, took Mike's weight across his shoulders, careful not to bash into his mashed leg, and stood tall.

Making his way forward into the ever-darkening night, he did a quick bit of maths. With Mike's kit, including his rifle, that was at least an extra fifteen kilos he was carrying. He put Mike at around twelve stone, which was another seventy-six kilos. Give or take a few kilos, that meant he was now trying to outrun the Taliban carrying another ninety kilos on his back, at night, and with no idea where he was, or how he was going to get back to the compound. Things weren't exactly looking good, but worrying wasn't going to make any difference. He just had to focus on digging deep and getting them out of the shit.

An hour later, having stopped after half an hour for a rest to get his breath back and neck some water, Liam knew he'd covered barely a mile. Regardless, it was time to call it a day and he'd spotted what he hoped would be a decent place to hide out. His back was in bits, his legs were probably two inches shorter, and it was so dark now that he was in serious danger of putting a foot wrong and doing himself an injury. And he had no idea if he was within one step or two hundred of an IED. The one good thing was that Mike had passed out, the only sign that he was still alive being the warmth of his breath against Liam's arm.

Placing him on the ground, Liam stretched out his back then crept over to where they were going to hide. If it was crap, it would still have to do. They could go no further.

It was a patch of bush so thick he couldn't find a way in, but he had to work something out because staying out in the open was just plain stupid. Quickly he pulled out his knife and discovered that its razor-like blade cut through the bush with ease. Within minutes, Liam had carved out a tunnel leading to the centre of the bush, which to his surprise was a lot less thick. Clearing an area for them to kip down on, he slipped back out for

Mike, then dragged him into the centre of the bush, laying him down on some dried leaves he'd managed to collect from around and about. Then he grabbed their kit. The last thing he did was to tie together a great thick bunch of the bits he'd cut from the bush. Then as he slipped back in to lie beside Mike, he pulled it in behind him, effectively bunging up the entrance. Liam had no idea if it would work, or if it was just wishful thinking, but it was the best he could come up with and, with the cover of darkness, at least they'd be hidden until first light.

Getting his head down, he thought it would be impossible to sleep, what with everything that had happened and was happening right now. But when he woke hours later to a sky just colouring with the morning, he was both surprised and pleased. Not only had he slept, but he felt refreshed for it. Now, though, they had to move.

Sitting up, Liam gave Mike a nudge. The soldier groaned, opened his eyes. He was pale, almost to the point of being grey. Liam checked him over again, changed his bandages, cleaned the wound as best he could, and topped up Mike's dose of painkillers. He then forced him to get some food down his neck. It wasn't much, just a pouch of burger and beans from a twenty-four-hour ration pack they all carried, washed down with water, but they both needed the energy for whatever the day ahead held for them.

A sound froze Liam's blood, and he looked at Mike, whose eyes were wide and white and staring.

'Don't move,' whispered Liam, and slowly, carefully, shuffled so that he could stare out through the bush and see what had made the sound.

The first thing he noticed was that his hideout for the night had been a good choice. He could hardly see out, which meant that anyone looking in would be hard pushed to spot them. And his bunging up of their entrance had also worked well. But he had no time to feel smug. He still hadn't worked out what had made the sound.

It came again, closer this time. A dull, metallic ringing. Then Liam saw the source of the sound: a couple of goats, and behind them a small boy. He must've been no older than eight, thought Liam, as the boy drew closer.

'What is it?' Mike whispered.

Liam held up a hand to shush him.

The goats came closer. Liam willed them to continue on, but they didn't. A few steps more and they were munching on the bush, right where Liam and Mike had crept in.

The boy approached. He couldn't see them, Liam was sure of it. But then something caught the boy's attention. He shuffled closer to the bush, crouched down, then reached out a hand and touched the paracord Liam had used to tie together the plug of bush he'd dragged in after them.

The boy looked up and stared right into Liam's eyes.

24

'Shoot him . . .'

Liam looked across at Mike, whose eyes were filled not just with fear, but with a calculated coldness.

'You have to shoot him, Liam,' Mike repeated. 'It's him or us.'

Liam shook his head. He knew that if the boy ran home, they'd be pinged in minutes, and the Taliban would come down on them hard and fast. There would be no escape. He also knew there was no way in hell he could kill an innocent kid.

'You know what will happen to us if you're caught, don't you, Liam?' Mike continued, propping himself up on his arm. 'There will be no chance of escape. And the last thing anyone will see of us is a little home-made movie of our deaths.'

Liam turned back to the boy. He was still staring, but he didn't look exactly afraid; more intrigued.

'I'm not going to shoot him,' said Liam. 'So you can just shut that idea down right now.'

'You've no choice,' said Mike, but Liam was ignoring him and instead pushing out the thick plug of bush to go and see the boy.

The boy backed off, but his goats were more inquisitive and took a nibble of Liam's trousers.

Liam forced himself to remember the few words of Pashto he'd learned over the past weeks.

'*Salaam alaikum*,' he said, and smiled.

The boy smiled.

Well, that's hello, thought Liam and said, '*Zma num* Liam.'

'*Salaam*, Liam,' said the boy, then pointed at Mike. Liam hadn't a clue what he said next, so he just answered in English and attempted to mime how Mike had been injured.

The boy nodded, and Liam thought that his face looked too serious for someone his age. He briefly wondered just what the boy had already seen in so few years of being alive.

One of the goats nudged the boy. Liam stared at him, half expecting him to run screaming back the way he came. But instead, the boy smiled, waved, and just walked on by. Liam watched him go, relief overwhelming him.

'You're an idiot,' said Mike, his voice hoarse with pain. He was sweating too, and not just from the heat already creeping through the morning.

Liam didn't respond. Whatever Mike thought of him now, it couldn't be any worse than before. And there was no way he was going to put a bullet in a kid; not unless the kid was firing a weapon at him.

But the boy had found them and that was enough – they had to get out and move position. Liam was nervous about moving at all, though; without the cover of at least a dull evening, if not the thick darkness of night, they'd be much easier to spot. But they had no choice, couldn't risk staying put.

He sorted their kit out then looked at Mike. 'We've got to go,' he said, making it clear from the off that there was no arguing. 'We'll stick to gullies and ditches as best we can. As soon as we find a place to hide out in, we'll get out of sight.'

'We're fucked,' said Mike, his voice sounding as bruised as the rest of his body. 'What's the point?'

Liam seethed with anger. 'The point,' he snarled, leaning in close to Mike, 'is that no matter how much of a complete and total fucking arsehole you are, I'm not going to let you sodding well die on me!'

Mike shook his head and sneered.

'Dan is dead,' said Liam, grabbing Mike and forcing

him to listen. 'And I'll always blame myself for it. Cameron is dead, and I couldn't save him either. And now, whether I like it or not, with you I've got a chance. So deal with it!'

Liam poked his head out of the bush to check that they were OK. He eyed a gully they could get to, which led to good cover further on, then dragged Mike out, hoisted him onto his shoulders and headed off.

The gully was deep and once they were in it, they were completely hidden. It was a small consolation for moving in the light of day, and with each step Liam took, he became more and more conscious that the Taliban would still be out looking for them. And then there was the boy, but he couldn't afford to think about it; he still stood by his decision not to shoot him.

Carrying all the kit, and Mike too, Liam was forced to take regular stops. He rationed the water, but knew it wouldn't last much longer. Then it would be down to finding some that didn't look too hideous and dropping in some purifying tablets, which made it taste even worse, but he knew it would prevent them from dying of a deadly case of the shits.

Come the afternoon, Liam guessed he must have moved them four or five miles at least, but he was exhausted and couldn't go on much further. Even worse, he'd checked Mike's wounds and they were beginning to fester. The heat wasn't helping and he was running out of bandages. But he still wasn't about to give up. Like he'd said to Mike, he'd seen two people die and been unable to do anything about either of them. This time was going to be different. It just *had* to be.

At long last, evening rolled in and Liam was relieved that they'd somehow managed to avoid any contact. He didn't know whether to be relieved or disturbed, and wondered if the Taliban were just playing with them, tracking them for fun. One thing he was sure about, though, was that neither of them would last much longer. All the time they were moving, he was trying to keep them heading in the right direction, but he couldn't go on indefinitely. Thinking back to the flight out on the Chinook, it was almost impossible to have a clear idea of just how far they'd come. Liam was pinning his hopes on little more than being spotted by friendly forces, running into a patrol out searching for them. It wasn't much, but it was all he had.

With Mike resting on the ground, Liam took stock of where they were and where they could move to – which, judging by Mike's present state, wouldn't be much further.

'There's a compound about half a mile away,' Liam said. 'Looks deserted.'

'They all look deserted,' said Mike. 'Right up until

the moment you walk in and find yourself in the middle of a Taliban board meeting.'

'This one's hardly standing,' said Liam. 'Place is more rubble than anything else. But it'll give us somewhere to lie low.'

'To what end?' asked Mike. 'What's your plan, Liam? To walk me all the way back to Camp Bastion? I'll be dead within days, we both know it.'

'They'll be out looking for us,' Liam replied.

'So are the Taliban,' said Mike.

'Well, it's the best chance we've got. We just have to make sure we get found by our side first.'

Mike was quiet as Liam picked him up again. As Liam walked, Mike moaned with every step, but Liam didn't stop – he had to get them to the ruined compound. There was no other cover out here, and despite wanting to move at night, he knew that neither of them could go on.

When they arrived at the ruined buildings, it was clear that the place had been left to rot into the ground. It was a large structure, with numerous little sections all divided by walls competing with each other to crumble to the ground first, but the only tracks Liam could see were those of animals, and from the evidence in front of him the only reason they used it was to have a crap.

'I know we should keep moving,' said Liam, checking

Mike over again, 'but it's too dangerous. We've no idea where we're going and it's only going to be so long before we find another IED.'

Mike nodded, tried to speak, but winced.

'Pain's getting worse, isn't it?'

Mike nodded again and for a moment Liam thought he was about to pass out. Then he rolled forwards, falling onto his left-hand side. Liam only just managed to catch his head before it crunched into a large rock. Even though his muscles were already starting to seize up on him, Liam forced himself to get Mike into as comfortable a position as possible. That done, he sorted himself somewhere to lie down, checked again that they were hidden from view and closed his eyes.

A scream tore through Liam's head and he was woken immediately to an early dawn. It was Mike. He was sitting bolt upright and yelling out like he was being pushed through a wood shredder.

Liam grabbed him, wrapping his hands round Mike's mouth to shut him up.

'The hell you doing?' he hissed. 'Shut up! Shut up! Shut up!'

Mike struggled, kept screaming, squirming to get out of Liam's grip. Then he lashed out and caught Liam hard across the cheek. It stung and Liam lost his grip.

Mike, free of Liam, made to stand. As he did so, he collapsed back down with a bone-breaking thud that only served to make him scream even louder.

Liam didn't know what to do, or what was wrong. He grabbed at Mike, tried to calm him, but nothing worked. Mike's eyes were staring into another world and Liam knew that wherever he was, it wasn't in the here and now.

Desperate now, and scared, Liam slapped Mike hard in the face. 'Shut up! Just bloody well shut up!'

He slapped him again and Mike fell away from the strike, his scream knocked back to a tearful whimper.

Then, when Liam was about to ask what the hell he'd been thinking, he heard another sound. Voices.

And they were right outside the compound.

25

Liam dropped to Mike's side, pinned a hand over his mouth and hissed at him to be quiet. This time, Mike understood.

The footsteps were drawing closer, scuffling along in the dirt. The voices were speaking Pashto. Liam prayed they were just farmers. But if they were, why were they out in the dark? What were they doing?

They were so close now he was sure they could hear him breathing. A flickering light cut through the gloom of the dawn, and a few seconds later Liam smelled cigarette smoke in the air. It reminded him of Jason.

The voices started up again. From what Liam could hear from where he and Mike were lying, there were two of them. He just had no idea who or what they were. And that was the problem.

With little left that he could do, Liam kept Mike low and quiet. He relaxed his grip and found Mike's SA80.

He also found Mike's pistol and slipped it into Mike's hand with a nod. Like his own, it was an Army issue Browning High Power 9mm. Firing one was nothing like in the movies, where you could hit a moving target a hundred metres away. The kick from the pistol was hefty, but at close range it could stop a grown man dead.

Mike acknowledged Liam's actions, and for the first time Liam sensed that they were actually on the same side. Still, he hoped that what he was preparing for – a close-quarter scrap – could be avoided, and the two men would move off.

A laugh bounced out and was followed by the faint red glow of a cigarette ember being flicked high into the air. It flew over Liam, landing just a few metres short of Mike's face. And there it slowly died.

More movement, more footsteps. They were getting closer. Liam slipped his pistol up towards his chest and slowly and silently made the weapon ready. Then he eased it further up into the best possible firing position he could manage. It wasn't great, but it would have to do. He held his breath as a shadow swept into view not more than a metre away. Then he heard a familiar sound. Whoever the man was, he was now taking a leak. And he was close enough for some of it to splash against Liam and Mike. Liam was repelled by the sensation of it, and the smell, but he held it together, focused on keeping his breathing slow and steady, staying calm.

The man finished taking a slash and, without moving, lit another cigarette.

The flickering flame of the match the man used to touch the end of the tobacco was just enough to cast an orange glow over Liam and Mike's hiding place and turn the morning's gloom into a dull light. For a split second, Liam and the man stared at each other, both equally shocked. For Liam, though, the only thing he saw was the AK47 hanging at the man's side. And as the man made to pull the weapon up into position to shoot, Liam raised the pistol and fired three shots in rapid succession. The man dropped like he'd just taken a sledgehammer to the skull, toppling forward to smash what was left of his head open on the rocks between him and Mike. But Liam was given no time to process what had happened as another shadow appeared in front of them, only this one had his weapon up and was firing as he came in. But he had no idea what he was firing at, and thanks to the muzzle flash on the AK47 in his hands, Liam and Mike were able to pick him out easily. They both fired and the man dropped, just like his friend, dead before he'd hit the ground.

'Thanks,' said Liam, without even looking to Mike.

'Too close,' said Mike. 'Sure they were alone?'

Liam, pleased to see some spark in Mike again, said, 'I only heard two voices.'

'I don't believe they were just out here on their own,' said Mike. 'We have to move. Immediately.'

Liam agreed and scrambled to his feet, only to hear gunfire and drop to the ground again.

Rounds came in, thumping into the wall they were crouched behind. Then the firing stopped and they both heard footsteps.

Liam replaced the magazine in the SA80 as two more figures appeared in front of him. He opened up on them and they fell back the way they'd come in, rounds slamming into their chests, stopping them dead.

'This is it,' said Mike, though Liam noticed there was little emotion in his voice. He was just stating a fact, plain and simple.

'It's not over yet.'

Mike said, 'You're a stubborn bastard, Liam, I'll give you that. But I don't think waiting for the fat lady to sing is going to make any difference.'

More rounds came in, but this time from a different position. Somewhere in the compound itself.

Liam and Mike returned fire, neither exactly sure what they were shooting at.

'We're surrounded,' said Mike.

'Then why hasn't someone just dropped a grenade

in our laps?' asked Liam. 'It's easy enough, given where we are.'

'No idea,' said Mike. 'Not that it matters.'

Liam wasn't so sure. 'If we were dealing with a load of Taliban fighters, they'd just storm us, wouldn't they? There's only two of us and they'd overcome us easy.'

'What's your point?' asked Mike, as another blast of gunfire scattered hot metal into the walls around them.

'My point,' said Liam, 'is that I don't think there are many more to deal with. What grenades have you got?'

Mike handed over the four he had with him. 'You can't just lob them and hope for the best,' he said. 'But best of luck if that's what you're going to do.'

Liam checked Mike's pistol and handed him two full magazines so he had them close at hand just in case. 'You're going to cover me,' he said. 'When I move, you keep their heads down, you hear? And only stop firing when you hear the signal.'

'Signal?' asked Mike. 'What signal?'

'A loud bang and lots of screaming,' said Liam, and without another word, he jumped to his feet and started to run.

Gunfire chased him as he raced across the compound, away from Mike and at an angle to the bullets coming in. Then Mike was returning fire through the gap in the wall to his left and Liam knew he had to keep moving.

ANDY McNAB

The wall in front of him was probably two and a half metres high. Back home, free running, he'd have been up it without thinking, springing off the ground, getting a foot on the wall to help him on his way to grab the top. He hadn't made a move like that in such a long time now. It didn't matter, though; he had to make it. No choice.

Still sprinting, Liam landed a left foot on a large, flat rock and powered himself forward and into the air. He caught the top of the wall, his hands slipping a little, but he was up and over it so quickly it didn't matter.

Landing on the other side, he found himself in a small courtyard. To his right was a door leading out of the compound. The sound of machine-gun fire was coming from his right and behind him. The clatter of the AK47s was very distinct against the clean report of the SA80. He focused in on it, got a bearing on where it was coming from and decided on his route to get round behind the shooters.

Liam jumped up and sprinted again. The wall in front this time was shoulder-height and he leaped up with cat-like agility, grabbed it and swung his legs up and over to the left, landing on the other side ready to set off again, jumping across piles of rubble like they were little more than stepping stones. Despite the situation he was in, Liam could feel the smile on his face, not

240

just from the exertion and thrill of leaping and running and jumping but from the fact that he was free running for his life, in a tumbledown compound in Afghanistan. It was insane!

More gunfire, and Liam raced over another wall, this one at hip height, to bring himself behind the sound of the AK47s, dropping down behind a low wall, but not before he'd seen what he was up against. There were three of them, all armed and all completely oblivious to his presence.

Maximum aggression, that's what he needed right now; just as Corporal Burns had hammered into them back at Catterick.

Liam slipped two grenades out of his pockets, pulled the pins, swung round and lobbed them over hard, dropping immediately to the ground.

The shooting stopped abruptly, replaced by frantic, terrified shouts, which were then cut short by two explosions that chased each other up and out into the air.

Liam waited, but no sound came from where the grenades had gone off. He rolled over, then slowly stood, the SA80 at the ready. But there was no need. The three men were dead. The grenades had landed right in the middle of them and the effect had been dramatic. Unable to get away, the explosion had ripped the men apart. It was an awful, bloody sight and Liam, now that the adrenaline was spent, hurled. Wiping his mouth, he made his way back the way he'd come, only more slowly now, his head spinning from what had just taken place.

Mike was sitting up, pistol in his hand, but he saw Liam coming and lowered the weapon.

'What the hell happened?'

'There were three of them,' Liam answered. 'I managed to get round the back of them. Chucked in two grenades.'

'Dead?'

'Very,' said Liam, and slumped down next to Mike.

For a moment, neither soldier said a word. It had been a fast and furious firefight and they were both stunned by their own survival.

'You all right?' Mike asked, at last breaking the silence.

'I'm not sure I'll ever be all right,' Liam answered. 'But I'm alive, which is saying something, all things considered.'

Mike reached into a pocket and pulled out a bar of chocolate. He tore the top off and handed it to Liam. 'Easier to drink it in this heat,' he said, then nodded to where the Taliban had been firing from. 'You saved my life. Again.'

'I saved my own life,' said Liam, pouring the gooey

chocolate into his mouth. 'That you're still here is just an unhappy fucking coincidence.'

Mike attempted a smile but Liam saw a stab of pain snap it in two.

'So what now?'

Mike glanced up. 'How do you mean?'

'You tried to kill me,' said Liam, standing up now to look down on the injured Mike. 'That's something that sticks with you.'

Mike said nothing.

'Just because I'm saving your life doesn't mean I trust you,' said Liam. 'When we get back, I could have you court-martialled for what you did.'

'I know,' said Mike. He tried to say something more, but his voice simply dried up.

Liam chucked the chocolate wrapper on the ground. 'Fuck it,' he said. 'I'm still not going to let you die.'

'Glad to hear it,' said Mike.

'Don't be. When we get back, who's to say I'm not going to be a complete bastard?'

'Let's just get a move on,' said Mike. 'Someone will have heard this. Either that, or they'll notice that the five we've just killed are missing and send a party out to investigate.'

'Then we'd best get out of here,' said Liam. 'I'm not in the partying mood at the minute. You?'

'Agreed,' said Mike. 'And I'm not overly impressed with the venue. It's like they've not even made an effort.' He grimaced with pain as Liam helped him to his feet. 'You really think they're out looking for us?' he added.

'I have to,' Liam replied. 'It's the only thing keeping me going. We've probably got enough food to see us through another twenty-four hours, and that's only if we share it out. Water, if we find any, we can purify, but it still tastes like puke and will probably give us the shits no matter what we do. As for protection, we've got two pistols and a rifle and barely three mags between us. And you're a cripple.'

'It's not looking good, is it?' said Mike.

To that, Liam had no reply.

26

It was closing in on midday and Liam, for the first time since Mike had been injured, slipped and fell. He landed hard, his left knee smacking down badly onto a stone that stabbed into him and made him yelp like a kicked puppy. Somehow, he managed to keep hold of Mike, but only enough to lower him to the ground behind him.

'You OK, Liam?'

Liam gritted his teeth, then checked his knee. The rock had punched a hole through his combats and into his flesh, drawing a stream of dark blood. It looked like a small wound, but it was weeping like something much bigger.

'It's nothing,' he said, but when he got up, his leg was numb like he'd been sitting on it badly for a few hours and all feeling had gone out of it. The leg buckled beneath him and he dropped to the ground.

Mike reached over and shook Liam's right shoulder. 'You've got a dead leg,' he said. 'You need to give it a few minutes, then it'll be fine.'

'We haven't got a few minutes,' said Liam, rubbing his leg. 'We're out in the open, Mike. We have to get under cover.'

He looked ahead. The only reason they were out in the open at all was because the gully they'd been using had come to an abrupt end. With no other choice, they'd come out and made a run for it across a field to another ditch. They'd only got halfway when he had slipped and fallen.

'It's only another fifty metres and we'll be there,' he said, pointing ahead to where they had been heading.

Mike held him back. 'You can't stand on it yet,' he said, 'never mind lift me.'

Liam was angry. They'd got too far for it all to go wrong now. And then a sound clattered into the moment. Liam and Mike both fell dead silent, focusing on what they'd heard, trying to get a bearing on it as best they could.

'Helicopter,' said Mike. 'Search party?'

'Has to be,' said Liam. 'It's not going to be the Taliban, is it?'

The sound was drawing closer.

'Where the hell is it?' said Mike, shielding his eyes against the bright sky.

Then he saw it.

'It's a bloody Chinook,' he said. 'Look, Liam! Over there!'

Liam turned to look where Mike was pointing and saw the huge aircraft creeping through the sky like a fat beetle.

'It's coming this way,' said Liam. 'Don't suppose you've got a flare?'

Mike didn't get a chance to answer as the rattle of gunfire barged into the conversation.

'Where the hell's that coming from?' he asked, darting his head left and right. 'They're shooting at the helicopter!'

They both saw muzzle flash at the same time. It was coming from directly behind them. And whoever was firing was little more than a hundred metres away.

'They must've caught our scent,' said Mike.

Liam dropped to the ground and raised the rifle. 'Get your binos out and spot for me,' he said to Mike. 'If we make enough noise, perhaps the guys in the Chinook will hear us.'

Mike soon spotted one of the shooters. 'Left of that tall tree you'll see him. Drop him, Liam!'

A quick, three-bullet burst did just that, but at the same

moment an RPG was launched into the sky from an area further to their left. The rocket screeched overhead. The Chinook banked and the rocket missed by a mile.

Liam swung his weapon round to where the RPG had been fired.

'Two figures at nine o'clock,' said Mike, staring down his binos. 'They're readying another rocket.'

Liam found them, aimed, squeezed the trigger. The first bullets missed, but the second burst hit home at the very moment when the RPG was launched. Instead of blasting off towards the Chinook, it thunked into the ground not two metres from where it had started, then exploded in a deafening fireball.

Liam was given no time to gloat as more gunfire erupted around them. Following Mike's directions, he returned fire into a section of bush, emptied one mag, replaced it with a new one and kept on firing.

Behind them, the sound of the Chinook was growing louder. Then a new sound joined it as the area Liam had been firing into was slammed by such a fierce spray of ammunition that he ducked instinctively. When he looked up, trees and bush and dirt and rock were being shot to hell.

'It's the Chinook,' Mike shouted over the sound of the destruction, answering Liam's unvoiced question. 'M134 miniguns. Three thousand rounds a minute. Nothing's getting away from that alive.'

Liam nodded. When the weapon finally stilled, it was as if the world itself had stuck up its hands and surrendered. The sound of the Chinook's twin rotors thrummed behind them and Liam turned to see the helicopter dropping in low some one hundred metres away. The tailgate was lowered and in the back was a soldier manning an M60 machine gun, which was bolted to the floor. He waved at them both, urging them to get a move on.

'Looks like our lift's here,' Mike said. 'You ready?'

Liam stood up. His leg was still a little like jelly, but at least he hadn't collapsed again. He reached a hand down to Mike, who grabbed it, and he hauled him up again onto his one good foot.

From the back of the Chinook, a group of soldiers fanned out and started to provide covering fire. Liam didn't think anyone could have survived what the Chinook had just attacked with, but it was reassuring to know that they weren't taking any chances. Then he heard someone shout his name.

'Scott! Bloody well get a move on! Shift it!'

Liam hoisted Mike onto his shoulders, then turned towards the helicopter and pegged it. All he could see was that open tailgate waiting for him, growing larger the nearer he drew to it. Bullets were flying all around, but he was oblivious. All that mattered was reaching that aircraft and getting out of this safe.

He arrived at the helicopter and nigh on collapsed as he raced up the tailgate. Two soldiers caught him as his legs finally gave way while two others quickly got on with dealing with Mike.

The last thing Liam saw as the Chinook rose into the air, and before he passed out with tiredness, was the face of Sergeant Reynolds in front of him, grinning.

'You're a lucky bastard,' he said.

Then Liam's brain shut him down.

27

When Liam walked off the plane, it was raining. The sensation was like electricity tingling his skin. It was good to be back home, he thought.

After he'd gone through all the usual Army stuff, he headed back to barracks. With his first tour of Afghanistan over, he was still trying to deal with what had happened, and the fact that he'd survived. He couldn't remember the number of soldiers who had actually been killed on the same tour; one of them had been Cameron – that was more than enough for him to get his head round. Now, with a few months between him and what had happened, he'd finally started to move on. But that didn't mean it was forgotten. Something like that, and everything that had happened with Mike, was sure to stay with him for a long time yet.

Lying on his bed now, he was woken by a knock

rattling at his door. It was a big day, but he was tired. He was also not fully sure that he wanted any part of what was going to happen in London later.

'I'm assuming you're not going dressed like that.'

Liam looked up to find Paul White staring at him.

'You're getting a medal today, and I'm coming with you, or had you forgotten?' Paul opened Liam's wardrobe and pulled out his uniform. 'Get yourself showered and dressed,' he ordered. 'You've half an hour and then we're out of here and on a train. You can change into this when we get there, agreed?'

'Thanks,' said Liam, and stood up to take his uniform and put it in a suit carrier. 'Look,' he said, 'about Dinsdale . . .'

Paul held up a hand to stop Liam saying any more. 'Everyone knows what happened,' he said. 'We couldn't save him. You did everything you could. And so did I. Everything, mate. And that's all that really matters, isn't it?'

'That's not how it feels.'

'No one ever said it would,' said Paul. 'But we're soldiers in the best army in the fucking world – just like Cameron was – and we have to deal with it, just as he would have if it had been the other way round. Now shut the hell up and get dressed.'

* * *

By the early afternoon Liam was standing inside Buckingham Palace. At his side were Paul, Mike – who was refusing to sit in his wheelchair and was instead leaning on crutches – and his parents. Whereas his mum just looked pleasantly surprised, his dad, Liam thought, looked awkward, embarrassed almost, like he'd only just realized exactly what his son had achieved and still couldn't believe it.

Liam was called forward and a moment later found himself standing in front of the Queen. She leaned forward and pinned to his chest a medal – the Conspicuous Gallantry Cross.

'Well done,' she said.

Liam glanced down at the medal. The cross was of silver, mounted on a wreath of laurel leaves, and the ribbon was white, with narrow stripes of dark blue at each edge and a central stripe of crimson.

'Thank you, Your Majesty,' said Liam.

'You are a credit to yourself,' continued the Queen. 'And to your family and friends, and to 2 Rifles. You should be very proud.'

Liam stood back, bowed and then wheeled round and marched back.

'Dan would be proud,' said Mike, hopping over as Liam stood with his parents and Paul after the ceremony. He balanced himself, then reached out to shake Liam's hand. 'As would Cam, and as am I. I owe you, Liam.'

'So you've given up on trying to kill me, then?'

'Don't push your luck,' Mike replied. 'Wait till I get my new foot and we'll see!'

Liam didn't know what to say. After all he'd come from and then been through, to receive a medal – it was all too much.

At that moment he heard a voice call his name. When he looked up, he saw a man and a woman approaching and he recognized them immediately. Cameron's parents, there to collect a posthumous medal on behalf of their son.

'Liam,' said Cameron's father, reaching out to shake his hand, 'Cameron would have wanted us to congratulate you. He spoke of you a lot when he was on leave. Well done.'

'I'm sorry,' said Liam, his voice cracking. 'I did everything I could, I . . .'

Cameron's father squeezed his hand even tighter. Then they were gone.

For a moment, Liam watched them go. Then he looked down at the medal on his chest and remembered what Jason had said: that what mattered in the end was getting through each day and night, and heading home to a pint of beer, a warm bed and, if you were lucky, a shag. It made more sense now than ever before.

'Well?' asked Paul as rain started to fall. 'What now?'

'I guess two out of three isn't bad, is it?' Liam said.

Paul raised an eyebrow. 'What are you talking about?'

Liam smiled. 'Pint?'

ACKNOWLEDGEMENTS

FROM DIRECTORATE MEDIA AND COMMUNICATIONS, MINISTRY OF DEFENCE:
Lt Col Crispin Lockhart

FROM ARMY MEDIA AND COMMUNICATIONS:
Mr Charles Heath-Saunders
Captain Simon Vannerley

ASSISTANCE PROVIDED BY THE STAFF AND JUNIOR SOLDIERS OF:
The Royal Military Academy Sandhurst
The Infantry Training Centre, Catterick
The Army Foundation College, Harrogate

Also by Andy McNab

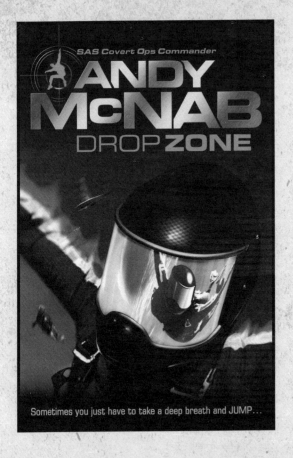

Everything changed the day seventeen-year-old **ETHAN BLAKE** saw a guy B.A.S.E. jump from the top of his block of flats. Now Ethan is part of the same elite skydiving team. But there's more going on than meets the eye. The team is involved in dangerous covert operations. In a life-or-death situation, does Ethan have what it takes?

Also by Andy McNab

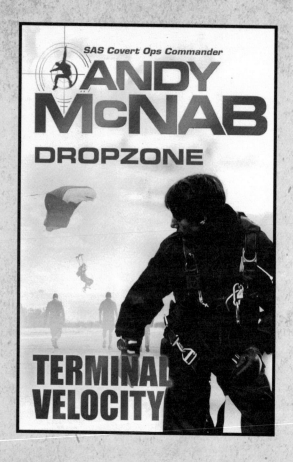

SAS Covert Ops Commander

ANDY McNAB

DROPZONE

TERMINAL VELOCITY

ETHAN BLAKE is back, and this time things are even more dangerous. As a member of a top-secret covert skydiving team, Ethan is being thrown into another high-stakes mission. His next assignment will take him straight to the enemy, where he will have to fight for his life.

Sometimes you just have to take a deep breath – and JUMP . . .